Husbands on Horseback

From the Outback of Australia to Texas soil—
follow the stories of two irresistible ranching men

Paper Husband Diana Palmer

Where is it written that a rancher's daughter has to
marry a long, tall Texan—or lose the ranch? In her
father's will—and Dana Mobry's just discovered that
her partner in this marriage of convenience is none
other than the sexiest cowboy in Texas, Hank Grant.
He insists they keep the marriage in name only, but
surrendering to temptation could transform a paper
husband into the love of a lifetime!

Bride in Waiting Margaret Way

One of the most influential and glamorous cattlemen
of northern Australia, Blake Courtland seems way out
of ordinary, hardworking Carolyn Donovan's reach.
A longtime neighbor, Blake has always been there
when Carrie has needed him most. But although the
air may spark between them, she is under no
illusions—Blake is not about to make his aggravating
neighbor his blushing bride....

Diana Palmer's first romance novel was for Silhouette Books in 1982. She is deemed to be one of the top ten romance writers in the country and is the winner of five national Waldenbooks Romance Bestseller awards and two national B. Dalton Books Bestseller awards. This is her first collaboration with Harlequin Books, writing about the American West, which she loves so well. Diana Palmer lives in Georgia, with her husband and son.

Margaret Way was first published by Harlequin Books in 1970—over twenty-five years ago—and she quickly became popular for her men of the Outback and her wonderfully evocative descriptions of Australia. She was born and educated in the river city of Brisbane and now lives within sight and sound of beautiful Moreton Bay in the State of Queensland.

DIANA PALMER
MARGARET WAY

Husbands
on Horseback

Harlequin Books

TORONTO • NEW YORK • LONDON
AMSTERDAM • PARIS • SYDNEY • HAMBURG
STOCKHOLM • ATHENS • TOKYO • MILAN
MADRID • WARSAW • BUDAPEST • AUCKLAND

ISBN 0-373-03427-X

HUSBANDS ON HORSEBACK

First North American Publication 1996.

Copyright © 1996 by Harlequin Books S.A.

The publisher acknowledges the copyright holders of the individual works as follows:

PAPER HUSBAND
Copyright ©1996 by Diana Palmer

BRIDE IN WAITING
Copyright ©1996 by Margaret Way

CONTENTS

Paper Husband
Diana Palmer

Dear Reader,

I can't possibly put into words what a privilege it is for me to share a book with my heroine, Margaret Way. Her *Red Cliffs of Malpara* was the very first Harlequin romance novel I ever read, and is the book that inspired me to write romance novels in the first place. I can't think of anyone in the industry whom I admire more, or who has given me more pleasure with her wonderful books.

This project is my first for Harlequin and I have enjoyed it more than I can tell you. I've spent a number of years kicking around sites in the American West, places like Tombstone, Arizona, and San Antonio and Fort Worth in Texas. I've been on ranches. I've seen how hard the cowboys work. I've eaten beef and beans, and I've seen ranches the size of eastern cities in Montana and Wyoming. I've loved the western states ever since I was a small girl and read Zane Grey's novels. I never dreamed that one day I, too, would have the privilege of writing books about the West and actually seeing them in print.

I hope that you enjoy the two stories contained in this volume. I know you are going to love Margaret's, because she's never written a book that wasn't wonderful. But I hope you like mine, too.

Thank you all for your loyalty over the long years. I have the greatest readers in the world. And I love every one of you.

Diana Palmer

CHAPTER ONE

THE SUMMER SUN was rising. Judging by its place in the sky, Dana Mobry figured that it was about eleven o'clock in the morning. That meant she'd been in her present predicament for over two hours, and the day was growing hotter.

She sighed with resigned misery as she glanced at her elevated right leg where her jeans were hopelessly tangled in two loose strands of barbed wire. Her booted foot was enmeshed in the strands of barbed wire that made up the fence, and her left leg was wrapped in it because she'd twisted when she fell. She'd been trying to mend the barbed-wire fence to keep cattle from getting out. She was using her father's tools to do it, but sadly, she didn't have his strength. At times like this, she missed him unbearably, and it was only a week since his funeral.

She tugged at the neck of her short-sleeved cotton shirt and brushed strands of her damp blond hair back into its neat French braid. Not so neat now, she thought, disheveled and unkempt from the fall that had landed her in this mess. Nearby, oblivious to her mistress's dilemma, her chestnut mare, Bess, grazed. Overhead, a hawk made graceful patterns against the cloudless sky. Far away could be heard the sound of traffic on the distant highway that led around Jacobsville to the small Texas ranch where Dana was tangled in the fence wire.

Nobody knew where she was. She lived alone in the little ramshackle house that she'd shared with her father. They'd lost everything after her mother deserted them seven years ago. After that terrible blow, her father, who was raised on a ranch, decided to come back and settle on the old family homeplace. There were no other relatives unless you counted a cousin in Montana.

Dana's father had stocked this place with a small herd of beef cattle and raised a truck garden. It was a meager living, compared to the mansion near Dallas that her mother's wealth had maintained. When Carla Mobry had unexpectedly divorced her husband, he'd had to find a way of making a living for himself, quickly. Dana had chosen to go with him to his boyhood home in Jacobsville, rather than endure her mother's indifferent presence. Now her father was dead and she had no one.

She'd loved her father, and he'd loved her. They'd been happy together, even without a huge income. But the strain of hard physical labor on a heart that she had not even known was bad had been too much. He'd had a heart attack a few days ago, and died in his sleep. Dana had found him the next morning when she went in to his room to call him to breakfast.

Hank had come immediately at Dana's frantic phone call. It didn't occur to her that she should have called the ambulance first instead of their nearest, and very antisocial, neighbor. It was just that Hank was so capable. He always knew what to do. That day he had, too. After a quick look at her father, he'd phoned an ambulance and herded Dana out of the room. Later he'd said that he knew immediately that it was hours too late to save her father. He'd done a stint overseas in the military, where he'd seen death too often to mistake it.

Most people avoided Hayden Grant as much as possible. He owned the feed and mill store locally, and he ran cattle on his huge tracts of land around Jacobsville. He'd found oil on the same land, so lack of money wasn't one of his problems. But a short temper, a legendary dislike of women and a reputation for outspokenness made him unpopular in most places.

He liked Dana, though. That had been fascinating from the very beginning, because he was a misogynist and made no secret of the fact. Perhaps he considered her safe because of the age difference. Hank was thirty-six and Dana was barely twenty-two. She was slender and of medium height, with dark blond hair and a plain little face made interesting by the huge dark blue eyes that dominated it. She had a firm, rounded chin and a straight nose and a perfect bow of a mouth that was a natural light pink, without makeup. She wasn't pretty, but her figure was exquisite, even in blue jeans and a faded checked cotton shirt with the two buttons missing, torn off when she'd fallen. She grimaced. She hadn't taken time to search for a bra in the clean wash this morning because she'd been in a hurry to fix the fence before her only bull got out into the road. She looked like a juvenile stripper, with the firm, creamy curves of her breasts very noticeable where the buttons were missing.

She shaded her eyes with her hand and glanced around. There was nothing for miles but Texas and more Texas. She should have been paying better attention to what she was doing, but her father's death had devastated her. She'd cried for three days, especially after the family attorney had told her about that humiliating clause in the will he'd left. She couldn't bear the shame of divulging it to Hank. But how could she avoid it, when it concerned him as much as it concerned her? Papa, she thought miserably, how could you do this to me? Couldn't you have spared me a little pride!

She wiped stray tears away. Crying wouldn't help. Her father was dead and the will would have to be dealt with.

A sound caught her attention. In the stillness of the field, it was very loud. There was a rhythm to it. After a minute, she knew why it sounded familiar. It was the gait of a thoroughbred stallion. And she knew exactly to whom that horse belonged.

Sure enough, a minute later a tall rider came into view. With his broad-brimmed hat pulled low over his lean, dark face and the elegant way he rode, Hank Grant was pretty easy to spot from a distance. If he hadn't been so noticeable, the horse, Cappy, was. Cappy was a palomino with impeccable bloodlines, and he brought handsome fees at stud. He was remarkably gentle for an ungelded horse, although he could become nervous at times. Still, he wouldn't allow anyone except Hank on his back.

As Hank reined in beside her prone body, she could see the amused indulgence in his face before she heard it in his deep voice.

"Again?" he asked with resignation, obviously recalling the other times he'd had to rescue her.

"The fence was down," she said belligerently, blowing a strand of blond hair out of her mouth. "And that stupid fence tool needs hands like a wrestler's to work it!"

"Sure it does, honey," he drawled, crossing his forearms over the pommel. "Fences don't know beans about the women's liberation movement."

"Don't you start that again," she muttered.

His mouth tugged up. "Aren't you in a peachy position to be throwing out challenges?" he murmured dryly, and his dark eyes saw far too much as they swept over her body. For just an instant, something flashed in them when they came to rest briefly on the revealed curves of her breasts.

She moved uncomfortably. "Come on, Hank, get me loose," she pleaded, wriggling. "I've been stuck here since nine o'clock and I'm dying for something to drink. It's so hot."

"Okay, kid." He swung out of the saddle and threw Cappy's reins over his head, leaving him to graze nearby. He squatted by her trapped legs. His worn jeans pulled tight against the long, powerful muscles of his legs and she had to grit her teeth against the pleasure it gave her just to look at him. Hank was handsome. He had that sort of masculine beauty about him that made even older women sigh when they saw him. He had a rider's lean and graceful look, and a face that an advertising agency would have loved. But he was utterly unaware of his own attractions. His wife had run out on him ten years before, and he'd never wanted to marry anyone else since the divorce. It was well-known in the community that Hank had no use for a woman except in one way. He was discreet and tight-lipped about his liaisons, and only Dana seemed to know that he had them. He was remarkably outspoken with her. In fact, he talked to her about private things that he shared with nobody else.

He was surveying the damage, his lips pursed thoughtfully, before he began to try to untangle her from the barbed wire with gloved hands. Hank was methodical in everything he did, single-minded and deliberate. He never acted rashly. It was another trait that didn't go unnoticed.

"Nope, that won't do," he murmured and reached into his pocket. "I'm going to have to cut this denim to get you loose, honey. I'm sorry. I'll replace the jeans."

She blushed. "I'm not destitute yet!"

He looked down into her dark blue eyes and saw the color in her cheeks. "You're so proud, Dana. You'd never ask for help, not if it meant you starved to death." He flipped open his pocketknife. "I guess that's why we get along so well. We're alike in a lot of ways."

"You're taller than I am, and you have black hair. Mine's blond," she said pointedly.

He grinned, as she knew he would. He didn't smile much, especially around other people. She loved the way his eyes twinkled when he smiled.

"I wasn't talking about physical differences," he explained unnecessarily. He cut the denim loose from the wire. It was a good thing he was wearing gloves, because the barbed-wire was sharp and treacherous. "Why don't you use electrified fence like modern ranchers?"

"Because I can't afford it, Hank," she said simply.

He grimaced. He freed the last strand and pulled her into a sitting position, which was unexpectedly intimate. Her blouse fell open when she leaned forward and, like any male, he filled his eyes with the sight of her firm, creamy breasts, their tips hard and mauve against the soft pink mounds. He caught his breath audibly.

Embarrassed, she grasped the edges of her shirt and pulled them together, flushing. She couldn't meet his eyes. But she was aware of his intent stare, of the smell of leather and faint cologne that clung to his skin, of the clean smell of his long-sleeve chambray shirt. Her eyes fell to the opening at his throat, where thick black hair was visible. She'd never seen Hank without his shirt. She'd always wanted to.

His lean hand smoothed against her cheek and his thumb pressed her rounded chin up. His eyes searched her shy ones. "And that's what I like best about you," he said huskily. "You don't play. Every move you make is honest." He held her gaze. "I wouldn't be much of a man if I'd turned my eyes away. Your breasts are beautiful, like pink marble with hard little tips that make me feel very masculine. You shouldn't be ashamed of a natural reaction like that."

She wasn't quite sure what he meant. "Natural...reaction?" she faltered, wide-eyed.

He frowned. "Don't you understand?"

She didn't. Her life had been a remarkably sheltered one. She'd first discovered her feelings for Hank when she was just seventeen, and she'd never looked at anyone else. She'd only dated two boys. Both of them had been shy and a little nervous with her, and when one of them had kissed her, she'd found it distasteful.

She did watch movies, some of which were very explicit. But they didn't explain what happened to people physically, they just showed it.

"No," she said finally, grimacing. "Well, I'm hopeless, I guess. I don't date, I haven't got time to read racy novels . . . !"

He was watching her very closely. "Some lessons carry a high price. But it's safe enough with me. Here."

He took her own hand and, shockingly, eased the fabric away from her breast and put her fingers on the hard tip. He watched her body as he did it, which made the experience even more sensual.

"Desire causes it," he explained quietly. "A man's body swells where he's most a man. A woman's breasts swell and the tips go hard. It's a reaction that comes from excitement, and nothing at all to be ashamed of."

She was barely breathing. She knew her face was flushed, and her heart was beating her to death. She was sitting in the middle of an open field, letting Hank look at her breasts and explain desire to her. The whole thing had a fantasy quality that made her wide-eyed.

He knew it. He smiled. "You're pretty," he said gently, removing her hand and tugging the edges of the blouse back together. "Don't make heavy weather of it. It's natural, isn't it, with us? It always has been. That's why I can talk to you so easily about the most intimate things." He frowned slightly. "I wanted my wife all the time, did I ever tell you? She taunted me and made me crazy to have her, so that I'd do anything for it. But I wasn't rich enough to suit her. My best friend hit it big in real estate and she was all over him like a duck on a bug. I don't think she ever looked back when she left me, but I didn't sleep for weeks, wanting her. I still want her, from time to time." He sighed roughly. "And now she's coming back, she and Bob. They're going to be in town for a few weeks while he gets rid of all his investments. He's retiring, and he wants to sell me his racehorse. Hell of a gall, isn't it?" he muttered coldly.

She felt his pain and didn't dare let him see how much it disturbed her. "Thanks for untangling me," she said breathlessly, to divert him, and started to get up.

His hand stayed her. He looked studious and calculating. "Don't. I want to try something."

His fingers went to the snaps of his chambray shirt and he unfastened it all down his chest, pulling the shirttail out of his jeans as he went. His chest was broad and tanned, thick with hair, powerfully muscled.

"What are you doing?" she whispered, startled.

"I told you. I want to try something." He drew her up on her knees, and unfastened the remaining buttons on her shirt. He looked searchingly at her expression. She was too shocked to protest, and then he pulled her close, letting her feel for the first time in her life the impact of a man's seminudity against her own.

Her sharp breath was audible. There was wonder in her eyes as she lifted them to his in fascinated curiosity.

His hands went to her rib cage and he drew her lazily, sensuously, against that rough cushion of his chest. It tickled her breasts and made the tips go harder. She grasped his shoulders, biting in with her nails involuntarily as all her dreams seemed to come true at once. His eyes were blazing with dark fires. They fell to her mouth and he bent toward her.

She felt the hard warmth of his lips slowly burrow into hers, parting them, teasing them. She held her breath, tasting him like some rare wine. Dimly she felt his hand go between them and tenderly caress one swollen breast. She gasped again, and his head lifted so that he could see her eyes.

His thumb rippled over the hard tip and she shivered all over, helpless in his embrace.

"Yes," he whispered absently, "that's exactly what I thought. I could lay you down right here, right now."

She barely heard him. Her heart was shaking her. His fingers touched her, teased her body. It arched toward him, desperate not to lose the contact.

His eyes were all over her face; her bare breasts pressed so close against him. He felt the touch all the way to his soul. "I want you," he said quietly.

She sobbed, because it shouldn't have been like this. Her own body betrayed her, giving away all its hard-kept secrets.

But there was a hesitation in him. His hand stilled on her breast, his mouth hovered over hers as his dark eyes probed, watched.

"You're still a virgin, aren't you?" he asked roughly.

She swallowed, her lips swollen from the touch of his.

He shook her gently. "Tell me!"

She bit her lower lip and looked at his throat. She could see the pulse hammering there. "You knew that already." She ground out the words.

He didn't seem to breathe for a minute, then there was a slow, ragged exhaling of breath. He wrapped her up in his arms and sat holding her close, rocking her, his face buried in her hot throat, against her quick pulse.

"Yes. I just wanted to be sure," he said after a minute. He released her inch by inch and smiled ruefully as he fastened her blouse again.

She let him, dazed. Her eyes clung to his as if they were looking for sanity.

Her mouth was swollen. Her eyes were as round as dark blue saucers in a face livid with color. In that moment she was more beautiful than he'd ever known her to be.

"No harm done," he said gently. "We've learned a little more about each other than we knew before. It won't change anything. We're still friends."

He made it sound like a question. "Of... of course," she stammered.

He stood up, refastening his own shirt and tucking it back in as he looked at her with a new expression. *Possession*. Yes, that was it. He looked as if she belonged to him now. She didn't understand the look or her own reaction to it.

She scrambled to her feet, moving them to see if anything hurt.

"The wire didn't break the skin, fortunately for you," he said. "Those jeans are heavy, tough fabric. But you need a tetanus shot, just the same. If you haven't had one, I'll drive you into town to get one."

"I had one last year," she said, avoiding his eyes as she started toward Bess, who was eyeing the stallion a little too curiously. "You'd better get Cappy before he gets any ideas."

He caught Cappy's bridle and had to soothe him. "You'd better get her out of here while you can," he advised. "I didn't think you'd be riding her today or I wouldn't have brought Cappy. You usually ride Toast."

She didn't want to tell him that Toast had been sold to help settle one of her father's outstanding debts.

He watched her swing into the saddle and he did likewise, keeping the stallion a good distance away. The urge to mate wasn't only a human thing.

"I'll be over to see you later," he called to her. "We've got some things to talk over."

"Like what?" she asked.

But Hank didn't answer. Cappy was fidgeting wildly as he tried to control the stallion. "Not now. Get her home!"

She turned the mare and galloped toward the ranch, forgetting the fence in her headlong rush. She'd have to come back later. At least she could get out of the sun and get something cold to drink now.

Once she was back in the small house, she looked at herself in the bathroom mirror after a shower and couldn't believe she was the same woman who'd gone out into the pasture only this morning. She looked so different. There was something new in her eyes, something more feminine, mysterious and secretive. She felt all over again the slow, searching touch of Hayden Grant's hard fingers and blushed.

There had been a rare and beautiful magic between them out there in the field. She loved him so much. There had been no other man's touch on her body, never another man in her heart. But how was he going to react when he knew the contents of her father's will? He didn't want to marry again. He'd said so often enough. And although he and Dana had been friends for a long time, he'd drawn back at once when he made her admit her innocence. He'd wanted an affair, obviously, but discovered that it would be impossible to justify that with his conscience. He couldn't seduce an innocent woman.

She went into her bedroom and put on blue slacks and a knit shirt, leaving her freshly washed and dried hair loose around her shoulders. He'd said they would talk later. Did that mean he'd heard gossip about the will? Was he going to ask her to challenge it?

She had no idea what to expect. Perhaps it was just as well. She'd have less time to worry.

She walked around the living room, her eyes on the sad, shabby furniture that she and her father had bought so many years ago. There hadn't been any money in the past year for reupholstery or new frills. They'd put everything into those few head of beef cattle and the herd sire. But the cattle market was way down and if a bad winter came, there would be no way to afford to buy feed. She had to plant plenty of hay and corn to get through the winter. But their best hand had quit on her father's death, and now all she had were two part-time helpers, whom she could barely afford to pay. A blind woman could see that she wouldn't be able to keep going now.

She could have wept for her lost chances. She had no education past high school, no real way to make a living. All she knew was how to pull calves and mix feed and sell off stock. She went to the auctions and knew how to bid, how to buy, how to pick cattle for conformation. She knew much less about horses, but that hardly mattered. She only had one left and the part-time man kept Bess—and Toast, until he was sold—groomed and fed and watered. She did at least know how to saddle the beast. But to Dana, a horse was a tool to use with cattle. Hayden cringed when she said that. He had purebred palominos and loved every one of them. He couldn't understand anyone not loving horses as much as he did.

Oddly, though, it was their only real point of contention. In most other ways, they agreed, even on politics and religion. And they liked the same television programs. She smiled, remembering how many times they'd shared similar enthusiasms for weekly series, especially science fiction ones.

Hank had been kind to her father, too, and so patient when a man who'd given his life to being a country gentleman was suddenly faced with learning to be a rancher at the age of fifty-five. It made Dana sad to think how much longer her father's life might have been if he'd taken up a less exhaustive profession. He'd had a good brain, and so much still to give.

She fixed a light lunch and a pot of coffee and thought about going back out to see about that downed fence. But another disaster would just be too much. She was disaster-prone when Hank was anywhere near her, and she seemed to be rapidly getting that way even when he wasn't. He'd rescued her from mad bulls, trapped feet in corral fences, once from a rattlesnake and twice from falling bales of hay. He must be wondering if there wasn't some way he could be rid of her once and for all.

It was nice of him not to mention those incidents when he'd rescued her from the fence, though. Surely he'd been tempted to.

Tempted. She colored all over again remembering the intimacy they'd shared. In the seven years they'd known each other, he'd never touched her until today. She wondered why he had.

The sound of a car outside on the country road brought her out of the kitchen and to the front door, just in time to see Hank's black luxury car pull into the driveway. He wasn't a flashy sort of man, and he didn't go overboard to surround himself with luxurious things. That make of car was his one exception. He had a fascination for the big cars that never seemed to waver, because he traded his in every other year—for another black one.

"Don't you get tired of the color?" she'd asked him once.

"Why?" he'd replied laconically. "Black goes with everything."

He came up onto the porch, and the expression on his face was one she hadn't seen before. He looked as he always did, neatly dressed and clean-shaven, devastatingly handsome, but there was still a difference. After their brief interlude out in the pasture, the atmosphere between them was just a little strained.

He had his hands in his pockets as he glanced down at her body in the pretty ruffled blue sundress.

"Is that for my benefit?" he asked.

She blushed. She usually kicked around in jeans or cutoffs and tank tops. She almost never wore dresses around the ranch. And her hair was long and loose around her shoulders instead of in its usual braid.

She shrugged in defeat. "Yes, I guess it is," she said, meeting his eyes with a rueful smile. "Sorry."

He shook his head. "There's no need to apologize. None at all. In fact, what happened this afternoon gave me some ideas that I want to talk to you about."

Her heart jumped into her chest. Was he going to propose? Oh, glory, if only he would, and then he'd never even have to know about that silly clause in her father's will!

CHAPTER TWO

SHE LED THE WAY into the kitchen and set out a platter of salad and cold cuts and dressing in the center of the table, on which she'd already put two place settings. She poured coffee into two mugs, gave him one and sat down. She didn't have to ask what he took in his coffee, because she already knew that he had it black, just as she did. It was one of many things they had in common.

"What did you want to ask me, Hank?" she ventured after he'd worked his way through a huge salad and two cups of coffee. Her nerves were screaming with suspense and anticipation.

"Oh. That." He leaned back with his half-drained coffee cup in his hand. "I wondered if you might be willing to help me out with a little playacting for my ex-wife's benefit."

All her hopes fell at her feet. "What sort of acting?" she asked, trying to sound nonchalant.

"I want you to pretend to be involved with me," he said frankly, staring at her. "On this morning's showing, it shouldn't be too difficult to look as if we can't keep our hands off each other. Should it?" he asked with a mocking smile.

Everything fell into place; his odd remarks, his "experiment" out there in the pasture, his curious behavior. His beloved ex-wife was coming to town and he didn't want everyone to know how badly she'd hurt him or how he'd grieved at her loss. So Dana had been cast as his new love. He didn't want a new wife, he wanted an actress.

She stared into her coffee. "I don't guess you ever want to get married again, do you?" she asked with studied carelessness.

He saw right through that devious little question. "No, I don't," he said bluntly. "Once was enough."

She grimaced. Her father had placed her in an intolerable position. Somehow, he must have suspected that his time was limited. Otherwise why should he have gone to such lengths in his will to make sure that his daughter was provided for after his death?

"You've been acting funny since your father died," he said suddenly, and his eyes narrowed. "Is there something you haven't told me?"

She made an awkward motion with one shoulder.

"Did he go into debt and leave you with nothing, is that it?"

"Well . . ."

"Because if that's the case, I can take care of the problem," he continued, unabashed. "You help me out while Betty's here, and I'll pay off any outstanding debts. You can think of it as a job."

She wanted to throw herself down on the floor and scream. Nothing was working out. She looked at him in anguish. "Oh, Hank," she groaned.

He scowled. "Come on. It can't be that bad. Spit it out."

She took a steadying breath and got to her feet. "There's a simpler way. I think . . . you'd better read Dad's will. I'll get it."

She went into the living room and pulled out the desk drawer that contained her father's will. She took it into the kitchen and handed it to a puzzled Hank, watching his lean, elegant hands unfasten the closure on the document.

"And before you start screaming, I didn't know anything about that clause," she added through her teeth.

"It was as much a shock to me as it's going to be to you."

"Clause?" he murmured as he scanned over the will. "What clause . . . Oh, my God!"

"Now, Hank," she began in an effort to thwart the threatened explosion she saw growing in his lean face.

"God in heaven!" He got to his feet, slamming the will back on the table. His face had gone from ruddy to white in the space of seconds. "What a hell of a choice I've got! I marry you or I end up with a stock car race-track on the edge of my barn where my mares foal! Moving the damned thing would cost half a million dollars!"

"If you'll just give me a chance to speak," she said heavily. "Hank, there may be a way to break the will—"

"Oh, sure, we can say he was crazy!" His black eyes were glittering like diamonds.

She flushed. He was flagrantly insulting her. She might love him, but she wasn't taking that kind of treatment, even from him. She got to her own feet and glared up at him. "He must have been, to want me to marry you!" she shouted. "What makes you think you're such a prize, Hank? You're years too old for me in the first place, and in the second, what sane woman would want to marry a man who's still in love with his ex-wife?"

He was barely breathing. His anger was so apparent that Dana felt her knees go wobbly, despite her spunky words.

His black eyes slewed over her with contempt. "I might like looking at your body, but a couple of kisses and a little fondling don't warrant a marriage proposal in my book."

"Nor in mine," she said with scalded pride. "Why don't you go home?"

His fists clenched at his side. He still couldn't believe what he'd read in that will. It was beyond belief that her father, his friend, would have stabbed him in the back this way.

"He must have been out of his mind," he grated. "I could have settled a trust on you or something, he didn't have to specify marriage as a condition for you to inherit what's rightfully yours!"

She lifted her chin. "I can hardly ask what his reasoning was," she reminded him. "He's dead." The words were stark and hollow. She was still in the midst of grief for the passing of her parent. Hank hadn't considered that she was hurting, she thought, or maybe he just didn't care. He was too angry to be rational.

He breathed deliberately. "You little cheat," he accused. "You've had a crush on me for years, and I've tolerated it. It amused me. But this isn't funny. This is low and deceitful. I'd think more of you if you admitted that you put your father up to it."

"I don't give a damn what you think of me," she choked. Her pride was in tatters. She was fighting tears of pure rage. "When you've had time to get over the shock, I'd like you to see my attorney. Between the two of you, I'm sure you can find some way to straighten this out. Because I wouldn't marry you if you came with a subscription to my favorite magazine and a new Ferrari! So I had a crush on you once. That's ancient history!"

He made a sound through his nose. "Then what was that this morning out in the pasture?" he chided.

"Lust!" she threw at him.

He picked up his hat and studied her with cold contempt. "I'll see what I can do about the will. You could contact your mother," he added pointedly. "She's wealthy. I'm sure she won't let you starve."

She folded her arms across her breasts. "I wouldn't ask my mother for a tissue if I was bleeding to death, and you know it."

"These are desperate circumstances," he said pointedly, a little calmer now.

"My circumstances are no longer any of your business," she said in a voice that was disturbingly calm. "Goodbye, Hank."

He slammed his hat over his eyes and went to the front door, but he hesitated with the doorknob in his hand and looked over his shoulder. She was pale and her eyes were shimmering. He knew she was grieving for her father. It must be scary, too, to have her inheritance wrapped around an impossible demand. If he didn't marry her, she was going to lose everything, even her home. He winced.

"Goodbye," she repeated firmly. Her eyes startled him with their cold blue darkness. She looked as if she hated him.

He drew in a short breath. "Look, we'll work something out."

"I'm twenty-two years old," she said proudly. "It's past time I started taking care of myself. If I lose the ranch, I'll get a grant and go back to college. I've already completed the basic courses, anyway."

He hadn't thought that she might go away. Suddenly his life was even more topsy-turvy than before. Betty was on her way back to town, Dana's father had tried to force him into a marriage he didn't want and now Dana was going away. He felt deserted.

He let out a word that she'd never heard him use. "Then go, if you want to, and be damned," he said furiously. "It will be a pleasure not to have to rescue you from half a dozen disasters a day."

He slammed the door on his way out and she sank into a chair, feeling the sudden warm wetness of the tears she'd been too proud to let him see. At least now she knew how he felt about her. She guessed that she'd be well-advised to learn to live with it.

The rest of the day was a nightmare. By the end of it, she was sick of the memories in the house. Grief and humiliation drove her to the telephone. She called Joe, the oldest of her two part-time workers on the ranch.

"I'm going away for a couple of days," she told him. "I want you and Ernie to watch the cattle for me. Okay?"

"Sure, boss lady. Where you going?"

"Away."

She hung up.

It only took her a few minutes to make a reservation at a moderately priced Houston hotel downtown, and to pack the ancient gray Bronco she drove with enough clothes for the weekend. She was on her way in no time, having locked up the house. Joe had a key if he needed to get in.

She spent the weekend watching movies on cable and experimenting with new hairstyles. She drifted around the shops downtown, although she didn't buy anything. She had to conserve her money now, until she could apply for a grant and get into college. On an impulse she phoned a couple of colleges around the area and requested catalogs be sent to her home address in Jacobsville.

The runaway weekend had been something of an extravagance, but she'd needed to get away. She felt like a tourist as she wandered around all the interesting spots, including the famed San Jacinto monument and the canal where ships came and went into the port city. Heavy rain came on the second day, with flash flooding, and she was forced to stay an extra day or use her Bronco as a barge, because the streets near the hotel were too flooded to allow safe travel.

It was late Monday before she turned into the long driveway of her ranch. And the first thing she noticed as she approached the farmhouse was the proliferation of law enforcement vehicles.

Shocked, she pulled up and turned off the ignition. "What's happened? Has someone broken into my home?" she asked the first uniformed man she met, a deputy sheriff.

His eyebrows went up. "You live here?" he asked.

"Yes. I'm Dana Mobry."

He chuckled and called to the other three men, one of whom was a Jacobsville city policeman. "Here she is! She hasn't met with foul play."

They came at a lope, bringing a harassed-looking Joe along with them.

"Oh, Miss Mobry, thank the Lord," Joe said, wringing her hand. His hair was grayer than ever, and he looked hollow-eyed.

"Whatever's wrong?" she asked.

"They thought I'd killed you and hid the body!" Joe wailed, looking nervously at the law officers.

Dana's eyes widened. "Why?"

"Mr. Grant came over and couldn't find you," Joe said frantically. "I told him you'd gone away, but I didn't know where, and he blew up and started accusing me of all sorts of things on account of I wouldn't tell him where you were. When you didn't come back by today, he called the law. I'm so glad to see you, Miss Mobry. I was afraid they were going to put me in jail!"

"I'm sorry you were put through this, Joe," she said comfortingly. "I should have told you I was going to Houston, but it never occurred to me that Mr. Grant would care where I went," she added bitterly.

The deputy sheriff grinned sheepishly. "Yeah, he said you'd had an argument and he was afraid you might have done something drastic...."

She glared at him so furiously that he broke off. "If that isn't conceit, I don't know what is! I wouldn't kill myself over a stuck-up, overbearing, insufferable egotist like Mr. Grant unless I was goofy! Do I look goofy?"

He cleared his throat. "Oh, no, ma'am, you don't look at all goofy to me!"

While he was defending himself, Hank came around the side of the house to see where the search party had disappeared to, and stopped when he saw Dana. "So there you are!" he began furiously, bare-headed and wild-eyed as he joined her. "Where in hell have you been? Do you have any idea how much trouble you've caused?"

She lifted her chin. "I've been to Houston. Since when is going to Houston a crime? And since when do I have to inform you of my whereabouts?"

He snorted. "I'm a concerned neighbor."

"You're a royal pain in the neck, and I left town to get away from you," she snapped. "I don't want to see you or talk to you!"

He straightened his shoulders and his mouth compressed. "As long as you're all right."

"You might apologize to poor Joe while you're about it," she added pointedly. "He was beside himself, thinking he was going to jail for doing away with me."

"I never said any such thing," he muttered. He glanced at Joe. "He knows I didn't think he'd done you in."

That was as close as he was likely to come to an apology, and Joe accepted it with less rancor than Dana would have.

"Thanks for coming out," Hank told the deputy and the others. "She was missing for two days and I didn't know where she was. Anything could have happened."

"Oh, he knows that," the city policeman, Matt Lovett, said with a grin, jerking his thumb at the deputy sheriff. "He and his wife had an argument and she drove off to her mother's. On the way her car died. She left it on the river bridge and caught a ride into town to get a mechanic.''

"Matt . . . !" the deputy grumbled.

Matt held up a hand. "I'm just getting to the best part. He went after her and saw the car and thought she'd jumped off the bridge. By the time she got back with the mechanic, the civil defense boys were out there dragging the river.''

"Well, she might have been in there," the deputy defended himself, red-faced. He grinned at Hank. "And Miss Mobry might have been eaten by one of her young steers.''

"Or carried off by aliens," Matt mused, tongue in cheek. "That's why our police force is always on the job, Miss Mobry, to offer protection to any citizen who needs it. I'd dearly love to protect you at a movie one night next week," he added with twinkling green eyes. "Any night you like. A good movie and a nice big burger with fries.''

Dana's eyes were twinkling now, too.

Hank stepped in between her and the policeman. "I think she'll need some rest after today's excitement, but I'm sure she appreciates the offer, Matt.''

The words didn't match the dark threat in his eyes. Matt had only been teasing, although if he'd really wanted to take Dana out, all the threats in the world wouldn't have stopped him.

"You're probably right," Matt agreed. He winked at Dana. "But the offer stands, just the same.''

She smiled at him. He really was nice. "Thanks, Matt.''

The law enforcement people said their farewells and went off to bigger tasks, leaving Dana and Joe and Hank standing aimlessly in the front yard.

"I'll get home now, Miss Mobry. So glad you're all right," Joe said again.

"Thanks, Joe," she replied. "I'm sorry for all the trouble you had."

"Not to worry."

He ambled off. Dana folded her arms over her breasts and glared furiously at Hank.

He had his hands deep in his pockets. He looked more uncomfortable than she'd ever seen him.

"Well, how was I to know you hadn't done something desperate?" he wanted to know. "I said some harsh things to you." He averted his eyes, because it disturbed him to remember what he'd said. In the few days Dana had been missing, he'd done a lot of remembering, mostly about how big a part of his life Dana was, and the long friendship he'd shared with her. He'd had no right to belittle the feelings she had for him. In fact, it had rocked his world when he realized how long he'd been deliberately ignoring them. He was torn between his lingering love for Betty and his confused feelings for Dana. It was an emotional crisis that he'd never had to face before. He knew he wasn't handling it very well.

Dana didn't budge an inch. "I've already decided what I'm going to do, in case you had any lingering worries," she told him coolly. "If you can find a loophole, a way for us to break the will, I'm going to sell the place and go back to school. I have catalogs coming from three colleges."

His face went rigid. "I thought you liked ranching."

She made an amused, bitter sound. "Hank, I can't even use a fence tool. I can't pull a calf without help from Joe or Ernie. I can feed livestock and treat wounds and check for diseases, but I can't do heavy lifting and fix machinery. I don't have the physical strength, and I'm running out of the financial means to hire it done." She threw up her hands. "If I even tried to get a job at someone else's ranch, with my lack of skills, they'd laugh at me. How in the world can I run a ranch?''

''You can sell it to me and I'll run it for you,'' he said curtly. ''You can rent the house and stay here.''

''As what?'' she persisted. ''Caretaker? I want more than that from life.''

''Such as?'' he asked.

''Never you mind,'' she said evasively, because a ready answer didn't present itself. ''Did you talk to my lawyer?''

''No.''

''Then would you, please?''

He stuck his hands into his pockets. ''Listen, Dana, no court in Jacobsville is going to throw out that will on the grounds that your father was incompetent. His mind was as sound as mine, and he knew business inside out.''

Her heart fell. ''He might have been temporarily upset when he inserted that clause.''

''Maybe he was,'' he agreed. ''Maybe he'd had some chest pain or a premonition. I'm sure he meant it as a way to make sure you weren't left alone, with no support, after he was gone. But his reasons don't matter. Either you marry me or we both stand to lose a hell of a lot of money.''

''You don't want to marry me,'' she reminded him with painful pleasure. ''You said so.''

He drew in a long, weary breath and searched her wan little face. ''God, I'm tired,'' he said unexpectedly. ''My life is upside down. I don't know where I'm going, or why. No, Dana, I don't want to marry you. That's honest. But there's a lot riding on that will.'' He moved his shoulders, as if to ease their stiffness. ''I'd rather wait a few weeks, at least until Betty's visit is over. But there's a time limit as well. A month after your father's death, I believe, all the conditions of the will have to be fulfilled."

She nodded miserably.

"In a way, it would suit me to be married right now," he reflected solemnly. "I don't want Betty to see how badly she hurt me, or how much I still want her. I might be tempted to try and break up her marriage, and that's not the sort of man I want to be."

"What about her husband?"

"Bob doesn't care what she does," he replied. "He's totally indifferent to her these days, and he's no longer a financial giant. I don't think it would take too much effort to get her away from him. But she left me because he had more money, don't you see?" he added pointedly. "My God, I can't let myself be caught in that old trap again, regardless of what I feel for her!"

She felt sorry for him. Imagine that. She linked her hands together over her stomach. "Then what do you want to do, Hank?" she asked quietly.

"Get married. But only on paper," he added deliberately, his dark eyes steady and full of meaning. "Despite the physical attraction I felt for you out in the pasture that day, I don't want a physical relationship with you. Let's get that clear at the outset. I want a document that gives you the right to sell me that land. In return, I'll make sure the figure you receive is above market price, and I'll put you through college to boot."

It sounded fair enough to Dana, who was wrung out from the emotional stress. "And I get to stay here, in my own house," she added.

"No."

Her eyebrows shot up.

"I'll want you to stay up at the homeplace with me," he replied, "as long as Betty and Bob are in town. Even though this is a legal marriage, I don't want Betty to know that I'm only a paper husband."

"Oh, I see," she replied. "You want us to pretend that it's a normal arrangement."

"Exactly."

She didn't want to agree. He'd hurt her feelings, made horrible remarks, insulted her and embarrassed her with today's womanhunt. But she needed to be able to sell the ranch. It would be her escape from the emotional poverty of loving where there was no hope of reciprocation.

"Okay," she said after a minute. "Will we have to get a blood test and a license at the courthouse?"

"We'll fly to Las Vegas and get married out there," he told her. "As soon as we've completed the legal maneuvers and Betty is safely out of my hair, we'll get a divorce there, which will be just as easy."

Easy marriage. Easy divorce. Dana, with her dreams of returned love and babies to raise, felt the pain of those words all the way through her heart.

"An annulment will spare you any hint of scandal afterward," he continued. "You can get your degree and find someone to spend your life with. Or part of it," he added with a mocking smile. "I don't think anybody has illusions about marriage lasting until death these days."

Her parents had divorced. Hank had divorced. But Dana had seen couples who'd stayed together and been in love for years. The Ballenger brothers with their happy marriages came instantly to mind.

"I'm not that cynical," she said after a minute. "And I think that children should have both parents while they're growing up if it's at all possible. Well," she added, "as long as it isn't a daily battleground."

"Was your family like that?" he asked gently.

She nodded. "My mother hated my father. She said he had no ambition, no intelligence, and that he was as dull as dishwater. She wanted parties and holidays all the time. He just wanted to settle down with a good book and nibble cheese."

She smiled sadly, remembering him, and had to fight the easy tears that sprang so readily to her eyes.

"Don't cry," he said shortly.

She lifted her chin. "I wasn't going to," she said roughly. She remembered him holding her at her father's funeral, murmuring comforting words softly at her ear. But he had little patience with emotion, as a rule.

He took a deep breath. "I'll set everything up and let you know when we'll go," he said.

She wanted to argue, but the time had long passed for that. She nodded. He waited, but when she didn't say anything else, he went back to his car, got in and drove away.

CHAPTER THREE

LAS VEGAS sat right in the middle of a desert. Dana had never been there, and the sight of it fascinated her. Not only was it like a neon city, but the glitter extended even to the people who worked at the night spots. Dana found the way women dressed on the streets fascinating and almost fell out the window of Hank's hired luxury car trying to look at them. It wasn't until he explained what they did for a living that she gave up her surveillance. It was interesting to find that what they did was legal and that they could even advertise their services.

"Here we are," he said gruffly, stopping at one of the all-night wedding chapels.

It looked flashy, but then, so did the rest of them. Hank offered her an arm but she refused it, walking beside him with her purse tight in her hand. She was wearing a simple off-white suit. She didn't have a veil or even a bouquet, and she felt their omission all the way to her toes. It was so very different from the way she'd envisioned her wedding day.

Hank didn't seem to notice or care. He dealt with the preliminaries, they signed a document, he produced a ring that she didn't even know he'd bought. Five minutes later, they were officially married, ring, cool kiss and all. Dana looked up at her husband and felt nothing, not even sorrow. She seemed to be numb from head to toe.

"Are we flying right back?" she asked as they got into the car once more.

He glanced at her. She seemed devoid of emotion. It was her wedding day. He hadn't given her a choice about her wedding ring. He hadn't offered to buy her a bouquet. He hadn't even asked if she wanted a church wedding, which could have been arranged. He'd been looking at the whole messy business from his own point of view. Dana had deserved something better than this icy, clinical joining.

"We can stay at one of the theme hotels overnight, if you like, and take in a show."

She didn't want to appear eager. The only show she'd ever seen was at a movie theater in Victoria.

"Well," she said hesitantly.

"I'll introduce you to the one-armed bandit," he added, chuckling at her expression.

"If you think we could," she murmured, and that was as far as she was willing to commit herself. "But I didn't pack anything for an overnight stay."

"No problem. The hotel has shops."

And it did. He outfitted her with a gown, a bag and everything in the way of toiletries that she needed. She noticed that he didn't buy any pajamas, but she thought nothing of it. Surely they'd have separate rooms, anyway.

But they didn't. There were too many conventions in town, and they got the last suite the hotel had—one with a king-size bed and a short sofa.

Hank stared at the bed ruefully. "Sorry," he said. "But it's this or sleep on the floor."

She cleared her throat. "We're both adults. And it's only a paper marriage," she stammered.

"So it is," he mused, but his dark eyes had narrowed as they assessed her slender, perfect figure and he remembered the sight of her in the pasture with her blouse open and the feel of her breasts pressed hard into his bare chest.

She glanced up, meeting that hot, intent stare. She flushed. "I'm not having sex with you, Hank," she said shortly.

His eyebrows went up. "Did I ask?" he drawled sarcastically. "Listen, honey, the streets are full of prime women, if I'm so inclined."

Her eyes blazed at him. "Don't you dare!" she raged. "Don't you dare, Hank!"

He began to smile. "Well, well, aren't we possessive already?"

"That's not the point. You made a vow. Until we have it undone, we're married." She stared at her shoes. "I wouldn't go running to some gigolo on my wedding night."

"Of course you wouldn't." He moved closer, his hands finding her small waist, and brought her gently to him. His breath feathered her forehead. "I can hear you breathing," he whispered. "Nervous?"

She swallowed. "Well . . . yes . . . a little."

His lips brushed her hair. "There's no need. It's a big bed. If you don't want anything to happen, it won't."

She felt disappointed somehow. They were legally married. She loved him. Did he really not want her at all?

He tilted her face up to his dark, curious eyes. "On the other hand," he said softly, "if you want to know what it's all about, I'll teach you. There won't be any consequences. And you'll enjoy it."

She felt the words to the very tips of her toes. But she wasn't going to be won over that easily, even if she did want him more than her next breath.

"No dice, huh?" he mused after a minute. "Okay. Suppose we go downstairs and try our luck?"

"Suits me," she said, anxious to go anywhere away from that bed.

* * *

So they went the rounds in the casino and played everything from the one-armed bandits to blackjack. The glittery costumes of the dancers on stage fascinated Dana, like everything else about this fantasy city. She ate perfectly cooked steak, watched the shows, and generally had a wonderful time while Hank treated her like a cherished date. In fact, that's what it was. They'd never been out together in all the years they'd known each other. During that one evening they made up for lost time.

They returned upstairs just after midnight. Dana had gone overboard with piña coladas, the one drink she could tolerate. But she'd underestimated the amount of rum the bartender put in them. She was weaving at the door, to Hank's patent amusement.

He slid the coded card into the slot and when the blinking green light indicated that it was unlocked, he opened the door.

"Home again," he murmured, standing aside to let her enter.

She tugged up the strap of her black dress that had slipped off her shoulder. Like the rest of her abbreviated wardrobe, it was the result of the afternoon's quick shopping trip. In addition to the knee-length cocktail dress and hose, she had a far too revealing black nightgown and no robe. She hoped Hank was agreeable to letting her undress in the dark.

"You can have the bathroom first," he invited. "I'll listen to the news."

"Thanks." She gathered her gown and underwear and went into the bathroom to shower.

When she came out, Hank was sitting on the edge of the bed. He'd removed everything except his slacks. He got up, and she had to suppress a shiver of pleasure at the sight of him bare from the waist up. He had muscular arms and a sexy dark chest with a wedge of curling black hair running down it. His hair was mussed and down on his forehead. He looked rakish because he needed a shave.

"Good thing I packed my razor," he mused, holding up a small pouch that had been in the attaché case he always carried when he traveled. "I have to shave twice a day." His dark eyes slid over her body in the abbreviated gown, lingering where her arms were crossed defensively over the thin fabric that didn't quite cover her breasts from view. "We're married," he reminded her. "And I've seen most of you."

She cleared her throat. "Which side of the bed do you like?" she asked shyly.

"The right, but I don't mind either one. You can have first pick."

"Thanks."

She put her discarded clothing on a chair and climbed in quickly, pulling the covers up to her chin.

He lifted an eyebrow. "Stay just like that," he coaxed, "and when I come out, I'll tell you a nice fairy tale."

She glared at him through a rosy haze. "I'll probably be asleep. I haven't ever had so much to drink."

He nodded slowly. "That may be a good thing," he said enigmatically, and went into the bathroom.

She wasn't asleep when he came out. She'd tried to be, but her mind wouldn't cooperate. She peered through her lashes and watched him move around the room turning out lights. He had a towel hooked around his hips and as he turned out the last lamp on his side of the bed, she saw him unhook the towel and throw it over the back of the vinyl-covered chair.

She stiffened as he climbed in beside her and stretched lazily.

"I can feel you bristling," he murmured dryly. "It's a big bed, honey, and I don't sleepwalk. You're safe."

She cleared her throat. "Yes, I know."

"Then why are you shivering?"

He rolled over and moved closer. She could feel the heat of his body through her thin gown. She trembled even more when his long leg brushed against hers.

"Shivering," he continued, moving closer, "and breathing like an Olympic runner." He slid a long arm under her and brought her sliding right over against him. "I haven't forgotten the signs when a woman wants me," he whispered as his hands smoothed the gown right down her body. "And you want me, Dana."

She started to protest, but his mouth was already covering hers. He turned and pulled her to him, so that she felt his nude body all the way down hers. He was warm and hard, and even in her innocence she was aware that he wanted her badly.

His lean hands smoothed over her flat belly, tracing down to the juncture of her long legs. His thumb eased between them and he touched her softly in a place that she hadn't dreamed he would.

She jerked.

"No," he said gently. "Don't pull back. This isn't going to hurt. It's only going to make it easy when I take you." His fingers were slow and sensual and insistent. She shivered, and the pressure grew. His mouth teased over her parted lips while he taught her body to yield to building pleasure.

"Does it feel good?" he whispered.

"Yes," she sobbed.

"Don't fight it," he breathed. His mouth slid down to her breasts and explored them in a silence that grew tense as the movement of his hand produced staggering sensations that arched her body like a bow.

He was doing something. It wasn't his finger now, it was part of his body, and he was easing down and pushing, penetrating...!

"It hurts," she whispered frantically.

"Here," he whispered, shifting quickly. He moved again, and she shivered, but not with pain. "Yes, that's it," he said quickly. "That's it, sweetheart!"

She was unconsciously following his lead, letting him position her, buffet her. She felt his skin sliding against her own, heard the soft whisper of it even as the sensations made her mind spin. She was making sounds that she didn't recognize, deep in her throat, and clinging to him with all her strength.

"I...wish...!" she choked.

"Wish what?" he bit off, fighting for breath. "What do you want? I'll do anything!"

"Wish...the light...was on," she managed to say.

"Oh, God..." he groaned.

He tried to reach the light switch, but just at that moment, a shock of pleasure caught him off guard and bit into his body like a sweet, hot knife. He gave up any thought of the light and drove against her with all his might, holding her thrashing hips as she went with him on the spiral of pleasure. He heard her cry out and thanked God that she was able to feel anything, because his only sane thought was that if he didn't find release soon, he was going to die...

"Dana!" he cried out as he found what he craved, shuddering and shuddering as he gave himself to the sweetness of ecstasy.

Her hands soothed him as she came back down again, shivering in the aftermath. She stroked his hair and his nape, pressing tender kisses on his cheeks, his eyes, his nose.

"It was good," she whispered. "It was so good, so sweet. Oh, Hank, do it again!"

He couldn't get enough breath to laugh. "Sweetheart, I can't," he whispered huskily. "Not just yet."

"Why? Did I do something wrong?" she asked plaintively.

He turned his head and kissed her soft mouth. "A man's body isn't like a woman's," he said gently. "I have to rest for a few minutes."

"Oh."

He kissed her lazily, stretching his strained muscles and drawing a deep breath before he laced her close against him again and sighed.

"Did it hurt very much?" he murmured drowsily.

"A little, at first." She stretched against him. "Heavens, it's just like dying," she remarked with wonder. "And you don't care if you die, because it's so good." She laughed wickedly. "Hank, turn on the light," she whispered.

"I thought you were a prude," he taunted.

"No, I think I'm a voyeur." She corrected him. "I want to look at you."

"Dana!"

"And don't pretend to be shocked, because I know you aren't. I'll bet you want to look at all of me, too."

"Indeed I do."

"Well, then?"

He turned on the light and peeled the covers away. She looked at him openly, coloring just a little at the sight of his blatant nudity. He didn't blush. He stared and stared, filling his eyes with her.

"God, what a sight," he murmured huskily. He held out his arms. "Come here."

She eased into them, felt him position her and lift her, and then bring her down over him to fit them together in a slow, sensual intimacy.

"Now," he whispered huskily, moving his hands to her hips. "Let's watch each other explode."

"Are we...going to?" she whispered back, moving slowly with him.

He nodded, because he couldn't manage words. His black eyes splintered as the sensations began to build all over again. His last sane thought was that he might never be able to get enough of her....

He was distant the next morning. Dana had expected a new and wonderful closeness because of their intimacy in the night, but Hank was quiet and reserved in a way he'd never been before.

"Is something wrong?" she asked worriedly.

He shrugged. "What could be wrong?" He checked his watch. "We'd better get a move on. I have an appointment in the office late this afternoon, and I can't afford to miss it. Got your stuff together?"

She nodded, still a little bewildered. "Hank...you aren't sorry about last night, are you?" she asked uneasily.

"Of course not!" he said, and forced a smile. "I'm just in a hurry to get home. Let's go."

And so they left and went home.

CHAPTER FOUR

DANA PEERED AGAIN at the thick gold wedding ring on her hand. They'd been back in Jacobsville for two weeks, and she was living in his big sprawling brick mansion now. The housekeeper, Miss Tilly, had been with Hayden for a long time. She was thin and friendly and secretly amused at the high-handed manner Hayden had managed his wedding, but she didn't say a word. She cooked and cleaned and kept out of the way.

Dana was uneasy at first. Her brand-new husband didn't wear a wedding band, and she didn't like to suggest it to him for fear of sounding possessive. But it made her uncomfortable to think that he didn't want to openly indicate his wedded state. Surely he wasn't thinking of having affairs already?

That was a natural thought, because despite his ardor in Las Vegas on their wedding night, he hadn't touched her since. He'd been polite, attentive, even affectionate. But he hadn't touched her as a lover. He was like a friend now. He'd insisted on separate bedrooms without any explanations at all, and he'd withdrawn from her physically to the point that he wouldn't even touch her hand. It wore on Dana's nerves.

His behavior began to make sense the next morning, however, when Tilly went to answer the doorbell and a strange couple entered the house as if they belonged there.

"Where's Hank? He saw Bob at the bank and invited him to lunch," the woman, a striking brunette, an-

46

nounced flatly. "Didn't he say he'd be back by this time, Bob?" she asked the much older, slightly balding man beside her. He looked pale and unhealthy, and he shrugged, as if he didn't much care. He glanced at Dana with an apologetic smile, but he seemed sapped of energy, even of speech.

"I don't know where he is. I just got home," Dana said. She was very conscious of her appearance. She was wearing jeans and boots and a dusty shirt, because she'd been down to her own place to check on her small herd of cattle. She smelled of horses and her hair wasn't as neat in its braid as it had started out.

"And who are you, the stable girl?" the woman asked with a mocking smile.

Dana didn't like the woman's attitude, her overpolished look, or the reek of her expensive perfume that she must have bathed in.

"I'm Mrs. Hayden Grant," she replied with curt formality. "And just who do you think you are, to come into my home and insult me?" she added for good measure, with sparks in her blue eyes.

The woman was shocked, not only by the name she'd been given, but by that quick hostility.

She fumbled her words. "I'm Betty Grant. I mean, Betty Collins," she amended, rattled and flushed. "I didn't know Hank... had remarried! He didn't say anything about it."

"We've known each other for years, but we've only been married a few weeks," Dana replied, furious at Hank for putting her in this position so unexpectedly. He hadn't said anything about his ex-wife paying a visit. "Tilly, show them into the living room," she told the thin housekeeper. "I'm sure Hank will be along," she added curtly. "If you'll excuse me, I have things to do." She spared the man a smile, because he hadn't been impolite, but she said nothing to Betty. Her feelings had been lacerated by the woman's harsh question.

She walked to the staircase and mounted it without a backward glance.

"She isn't very welcoming," Betty told her husband with a cold glance toward the staircase.

"She wasn't expecting you," Tilly said with irritation. She'd never liked the ex-Mrs. Grant and she liked her even less now. "If you'd like to wait in here, I'll bring coffee when Mr. Grant comes."

Betty gave the housekeeper a narrow-eyed look. "You never liked me, did you, Tilly?"

"I work for Mr. Grant, madam," she replied with dignity. "My likes and dislikes are of concern only to him. And to Mrs. Grant, of course," she added pointedly.

As the blood was seeping into Betty's cheeks, the housekeeper swept out of the room and closed the door. She went down the hall to the kitchen and almost collided with Hayden, who'd come in the back door.

"Whoa, there," he said, righting her. "What's got you so fired up?"

"Your ex-wife just slithered in, with her husband," she said grimly, noticing the pained look the statement brought to his face. "She's already had a bite of Mrs. Grant, which she got back, with interest," she added with a smile.

He sucked in his breath. "Good Lord, I forgot to phone and tell Dana I'd invited them. Is she very upset?"

"Well, sir," Tilly chuckled, "she's got a temper. Never raised her voice or said a bad word, but she set Betty right on her heels. Betty asked if she was the stable girl."

His face grew cold and hard. "How does she look?"

"Dana?"

He shook his head. "Betty."

"She looks very rich, very haughty and very pretty, just as she used to." She frowned. "Sir, you aren't going to let her knock you off-balance again, are you?"

He couldn't answer that. The memory of Betty in his bed had tormented him ever since the divorce, despite the ecstasy Dana had given him that one night they'd had together.

"No," he said belatedly. "Certainly I'm not going to give her any rope to hang me with."

"Might think about telling Dana that," Tilly mused. "She won't take kindly to the kind of shock she just got. Especially considering the sleeping arrangements around here."

He opened his mouth to reply hotly, but she was already through the door and into the kitchen. He glared after her. Tilly's outspokenness was irritating at times. She was right, which didn't help the situation.

"Bring a tray of coffee to the living room," he bellowed after her.

There was no reply, but he assumed that she heard him. So, probably, had half the county.

He strolled into the living room, trying not to think about how it was going to affect him to see Betty. He wasn't as prepared as he'd thought. It was an utter shock. She'd been twenty when she left him, a flighty girl who liked to flirt and have men buy her pretty things. Ten years had gone by. That would make her thirty now, and she was as pretty as ever, more mature, much more sensuous. The years rolled away and he was hungry for this woman who'd teased him and then taken him over completely.

She saw his reaction and smiled at him with her whole body. "Well, Hank, how are you?" she asked, going close.

With her husband watching, she reached up and kissed him full on the mouth, taking her time about it. She laughed softly when he didn't draw back. She could feel the tension in him, and it wasn't rejection.

He hated having her know how he felt, but he couldn't resist the urge to kiss her back. He did, thoroughly. His skill must have surprised her, because he felt her gasp just before he lifted his head.

"My, you've changed, lover!" she exclaimed with a husky laugh.

He searched her eyes, looking for emotion, love. But it wasn't there. It never had been. Whatever he felt for her, Betty had never been able to return. Her victorious smile brought him partially back to his senses. Ten years was a long time. He'd changed, so had she. He mustn't lose sight of the fact that despite her exquisite body and seductive kisses, she'd left him for a richer man. And now Hank was married. Dana was his wife, in every sense of the word.

He blinked. For the space of seconds he'd kissed his ex-wife, Dana had gone right out of his mind. He felt guilty.

"You look well," he told Betty. His eyes shifted from her to his friend Bob in the distance. He held out his hand. "How are you, Bob?" he asked, but without the warmth he could have given the man before the divorce.

Bob knew it and his smile was strained as he shook the proffered hand. "I'm doing all right, I guess," he said. "Slowing down a little, but it's time I did. How've you been?"

"Prosperous," Hayden replied with a faint, mocking smile.

"So I've seen," the older man said congenially. "You've made quite a stir among breeders, and I hear one of your two-year-olds will debut this year at the track."

"That's the long and short of it. How's the poultry business?"

"I've divested myself of most of my holdings," Bob said. He grimaced. "I was so busy traveling that I didn't realize I'd lost control until there was a proxy fight and I lost it," he added, without looking at Betty. "Then I had a minor stroke, and even my shares weren't worth the trouble. We're living comfortably on dividends from various sources."

"Comfortably is hardly the word," Betty scoffed. "But we've got one prize possession left that may put us in the black again. That's one reason we're here today." She smiled flirtatiously at Hank, who looked very uncomfortable, and deliberately leaned back against his desk in a seductive pose. "When did you get married, Hank? When you heard we were moving back here?"

His face hardened. "That's hardly a motive to get married."

"I wonder. Your new bride is frightfully young, and she seems to prefer the great outdoors to being a hostess. She wasn't very friendly. Is she the little farm girl whose father just died? She's not even in your league, socially, is she?"

"Oh, I wouldn't say that," came a voice from the doorway.

Hank turned his attention to his wife and didn't recognize her. Her blond hair was down around her shoulders, clean and bright, and she was wearing a silk sundress that even made Bob stare.

She was wearing just enough makeup, just enough perfume. Hank's eyes went down to her long, elegant legs and he felt his whole body go rigid as he remembered how it felt to kiss her. His face reflected the memory, to Betty's dismay.

Dana walked in, her body swaying gracefully, and took Hank possessively by the arm. She was delighted that she'd bought this designer dress to wear for Hank. The occasion hadn't arisen before, so she'd saved it. "I thought you'd forgotten the invitation," she said idly, glancing at Betty. "We're so newly married, you see," she added with indulgent affection.

Betty's face had flushed again with temper. She crossed her legs as she leaned back further into the desk. Her eyes narrowed. "Very newly married, we hear. I was just asking Hank why the rush."

Dana smiled demurely and her hand flattened on her stomach. "Well, I'm sure you know how impetuous he is," she murmured huskily, and didn't look up.

The gesture was enough. Betty looked as if she might choke.

Hank was surprised at his wife's immediate grasp of the situation, and her protective instincts. He'd been horrible to her, and here she was saving his pride. He'd been set to go right over the edge with Betty again, and here was Dana to draw him back to safety. Considering his coolness to her since their marriage, and springing this surprise on her today, it was damned decent of her.

His arm contracted around her waist and he smiled down at her with genuine appreciation. "A child was our first priority, but we sort of jumped the gun," he added, lying through his teeth as he helped things along. "We're hoping for a son."

Bob looked wistful while Betty fumed. "I'd have liked a child," he told them. "It wasn't on the cards for us, though."

"Children are a nuisance," Betty murmured. "Little irritations that grow."

"Aren't you lucky that your mother didn't have that opinion?" Dana returned smoothly.

Betty stood up. She'd been expecting a pushover, and she was getting one until the venomous child bride walked in and upset her cart. Things weren't going at all according to her plan. "Has Bob asked you about the racehorse? He hoped you might be willing to come down to Corpus Christi with us and take a look at him, Hank," she said, getting straight to the point. "He's a proven winner, with good bloodlines, and we won't rob you. We'll make you a good price."

Why hadn't he realized that Betty might have had an ulterior motive when Bob had all but invited himself and Betty for lunch? He'd thought she'd put Bob up to it because she wanted to see him again, perhaps because she'd regretted the divorce. But it was just like old times. She was after money and saw him as a way to feather her nest—and Bob's. Her body had blinded him again. Angrily he drew Dana closer. "I don't think Dana would feel up to traveling right now," Hank replied, continuing with the fiction of pregnancy.

"We don't have to take her with us," Betty said curtly.

Bob laughed. "Betty, they're newlyweds," he said with noticeable embarrassment. "What are you trying to do?"

"That would have been *my* next question, Mr. Collins," Dana replied quietly. "Although I'll tell you right now that my husband doesn't travel without me." She caught his hand in hers, and he was surprised at how cold it was, and how possessive.

"Oh, you don't surely think *I'm* after your husband," Betty scoffed. "I...we...only want to see our racehorse placed in good hands. Nobody knows thoroughbred horses like Hank." She shifted her posture, for effect. She had a perfect figure and she didn't mind letting it show whenever possible, if it was to her benefit. "You must be very insecure in your marriage, dear, if you don't trust your husband out of your sight with a married woman and her husband. And that's rather a sad statement about your relationship."

Dana flushed. She could tell that Hank was suddenly suspicious. He looked down at her with narrowed eyes, as if he'd taken Betty's taunt to heart. And his hand was dead in hers, as if he felt nothing when he touched her.

Dana felt his withdrawal. She drew her fingers away. So much for the pretense, she decided. "Hank and I have only been married for two weeks," she said.

"Yes, dear, but if you're pregnant, it hardly means you've only been sleeping together since you married, or can't I count?" she asked pointedly.

Which put Dana between a rock and a hard place. She couldn't admit that she and Hank had only slept together since their wedding, unless she wanted to make herself a liar about the pregnancy. She glanced at Hank, who'd started the fabrication, but he wasn't helping her now. In fact, he looked as if he hated being tied to her when Betty was within his grasp. Her husband didn't seem to be jealous at all. It was a frightening thought to a woman in love with a husband whose motives for the marriage had been suspect from the start, and who had admitted that he still felt something powerful for his ex-wife. He'd said, too, that he had no love to offer Dana; only affection.

"Besides, it isn't as if I'm trying to break up your marriage," Betty continued. "Bob and I are in terrible financial shape. That's one reason we're having to give up our holdings all over Texas and our racehorse. Even if Hank doesn't want to buy the horse, he might be able to help us find someone who'll want him. Surely you don't begrudge us a little advice, for old times' sake? It's only Corpus Christi, after all, not some foreign country. It would only mean a night away from home."

Hank was wavering, so Betty advanced on Bob and draped herself against him with a seductive smile, as if she was making him an offer. "Tell him, honey," she drawled seductively.

Bob's face burned with color as he looked at her and he shifted restlessly. "Come on, Hank," he said. "The stable where this horse is kept is right down the road, about ten miles from where we live. We've got plenty of room. You can spend the night and come back tomorrow." He smiled weakly. "We really can't afford to wait any longer. I've had some health problems, so I have to get this settled now. We were good friends once, Hank."

You're being suckered, Dana wanted to scream. *She's using him to get to you, she's bribing him with her body to coax you down to Corpus Christi so she can seduce you into buying that horse.*

Hank felt Dana's tension. His eyes narrowed as he looked down at her and recognized the jealousy, the distrust. He was feeling much too threatened already by Betty, and he was puzzled by the stormy indecision his own feelings brewed inside him. He felt trapped between two women, one whom he wanted to the point of madness and the other who'd discarded his heart and now seemed to want him again—despite her husband.

He glanced from Dana's set, angry face to Betty's coaxing one and felt himself wavering.

"Your wife doesn't have you on a leash or something, does she?" Betty asked pointedly.

That did it.

CHAPTER FIVE

MALE PRIDE asserted itself. "I can spare a day or two," Hayden told Bob with a meaningful glare down into Dana's flushed face. "After all, we're civilized people. And the divorce was years ago. It's stupid to hold a grudge."

Betty beamed. She'd won and she knew it. "What a nice thing to say, Hank. But you always were sweet."

Dana felt left out. The other two took over the conversation, and in no time, they were recalling old times and talking about people Dana had never met. She poured the coffee that a disgruntled Tilly had brought on a tray, with cake, and served it to the guests. But she might have been invisible, for all the attention Hank paid her. After a few minutes she excused herself and left the room, without being really sure that he'd even noticed her absence.

Tilly was headed toward the kitchen with her tray right ahead of Dana's retreat, muttering to herself about men who couldn't see their own noses. Normally Tilly amused Dana by talking to herself, but she was far too preoccupied today to notice.

She went up the stairs to the room she occupied alone and began to pack. If Hank was going away, so was she. She'd had enough of being an extra person in his life, in his house. If she'd had any hopes that he might one day learn to love her, they'd been killed stone dead with the arrival of his ex-wife. Anyone could see how he still felt about her. He was so besotted that he hadn't even noticed Dana once Betty flashed that false smile at him.

Well, let him leave with his ex-wife, on whatever pretext he liked, and good luck to him!

It took her ten minutes to pack. She threw off the sundress and put on jeans and a knit top and her boots. She braided her hair and looked in the mirror. Yes, that was more like it. She might have been a society girl once, but now she was just a poor rancher. She could look the part if she liked, and Hank surely wouldn't miss her if she left, not when Betty was ready, willing and able.

Apparently it didn't matter at all to Hank that Betty was still married, avaricious, and only using Hank to make a profit on that horse. God knew he could afford to buy it, and the woman looked as if she wouldn't mind coming across with a little payment in kind to reimburse him.

She was going through drawers to make sure she hadn't left anything when the door opened and Hank walked in.

He'd expected to find her crying. She had a sensitive nature and he'd been unkind to her, especially downstairs in front of their guests. Betty's remarks had made him feel like a possession of Dana's, and he'd reacted instinctively by shutting Dana out. Now he was sorry. His conscience had nipped him when she walked out with such quiet dignity, without even looking at him, and he'd come to find her, to comfort her, to apologize for making her feel unwelcome. But apparently it was going to take a little more than an apology, if those suitcases were any indication of her intentions.

"Going somewhere?" he asked politely, and without a smile.

"I'm going home," she said with quiet pride. "You and I both know that this was a mistake. You can get a divorce whenever you like. The will only required a paper marriage. The property is now mine and I promise you that I won't sell it to any enterprise that might threaten your horses.''

He hadn't been prepared for this. He stared at her with mixed feelings.

''It's a big house,'' he said, because he couldn't think of anything else to say.

''You and Tilly won't miss me. She's busy with domestic things and you're never here, anyway.'' She didn't meet his eyes as she said that, because she didn't want him to see how much his frequent absences had made her feel unwanted. ''I thought I might get a dog.''

He laughed coldly. ''To replace a husband?''

''It won't be hard to replace a husband who won't even sleep with me . . . !'' She stopped dead, cold, as she realized that the door was standing open and Betty was right there, listening.

Her abrupt cessation of conversation and her horrified gaze caused him to turn, too.

Betty wasn't even embarrassed. She smiled victoriously. ''I was looking for a bathroom. Sorry if I interrupted anything.''

''The bathroom's down the hall, as you know, third door on the right,'' Hank said shortly.

''Thank you, darling.'' Her eyes swept over the suitcases and Dana's pale face, and she smiled again as she left them.

Hank's face had no expression in it at all. Dana picked up her suitcase. ''I'll take this with me. If you wouldn't mind, could you have one of the men drop off the rest of my things? I've still got my Bronco in the garage, I hope?''

''I haven't done anything with it.''

''Thanks.''

She walked past him. He caught her arm, feeling the stiffness, the tension in her.

His breath was warm at her temple. "Don't," he said through his teeth.

She couldn't afford to weaken, to be caught up in some sordid triangle. Betty wanted him, and he'd always loved her and made no secret of it. Dana was an extra person in his life. She didn't fit.

Her dark blue eyes lifted to his brown ones. "Pity isn't a good reason to marry. Neither is breaking a will. You don't love me, any more than I love you," she added, lying through her teeth, because she'd always loved him. Her eyes lowered. "I don't want to stay here anymore."

His hand dropped her arm as if it was diseased. "Get out, then, if that's what you want. I never would have married you in the first place except that I felt sorry for you."

Her face was even paler now. "And there's the way you feel about your ex-wife," she returned.

He stared at her blithely. "Yes. There's Betty."

It hurt to hear him admit it. She went past him without looking up. Her body was shaking, her heart was bursting inside her. She didn't want to leave but she had no choice, it had been made for her. Even as she went down the staircase, she could hear Betty's softly questioning voice as she spoke to Hank.

Dana headed for the front door, and a voice called to her from the living room.

"Good Lord, you aren't leaving, are you?" Bob asked, aghast. "Not because of us?"

She stared at him without expression. "Yes, I'm leaving. You're as much a victim as I am, I guess," she said.

His mouth opened to refute it, and the sadness in his eyes killed the words. He shrugged and laughed shortly. "I guess I am. But I've lived with it for ten years, with taking Betty away from Hank with my checkbook.

Funny how life pays you back for hurting other people. You may get what you want, but then you have to live with it. Some choices carry their own punishment.''

''Don't they just?'' she replied. ''So long.''

''She doesn't really want him,'' he said softly, so that his voice didn't carry. ''She wants a way to live as high as we used to, on an unlimited budget. I've lost my bankroll so I've become expendable. It's his money she wants, not the man. Don't give up if you love him.''

She lifted her chin. ''If he loved me, I'd stay, I'd fight her to my last breath,'' Dana replied. ''But he doesn't. I'm not brave enough to have my heart torn out by the roots every day of my life, knowing that he looks at me and wants her.''

Bob winced.

''That's what you've done for ten years, isn't it?'' she continued perceptively. ''You're much braver than I am, Mr. Collins. I guess you love her so much that it doesn't matter.''

''It isn't love,'' he said coldly, with the most utter self-contempt she'd ever heard in a man's voice.

She sighed. The needs of men were alien and inexplicable to her. ''I guess we're both out of luck.'' She glanced toward the staircase with eyes that grew dark with pain. ''What a fool I was to come here. He told me he had nothing to give me. Nothing except wealth. What an empty, empty life it would have been.''

Bob Collins scowled. ''Money means nothing to you, does it?'' he asked, as if he couldn't comprehend a woman wanting a poor man.

She looked at him. ''All I wanted was for him to love me,'' she said. ''There's no worse poverty than to be bereft of that, from the only person you care about in the world.'' She made a little face and turned away. ''Take care of yourself, Mr. Collins.''

He watched her go, watched the door close, like the lid on a coffin. *Oh, you fool*, he thought, *you fool, Hank, to give up a woman who loves you like that*!

Dana settled back into her house without any great difficulty, except that now she missed more than just her father. She missed Hank. He hadn't been home much, probably because he was avoiding her, but at least he'd given her the illusion of belonging somewhere.

She looked at her bare hands as she washed dishes. She'd left the rings behind, both of them, on her dresser. She wondered if he'd found them yet. She had no reason to wear wedding rings when she wasn't a wife anymore. Hank had married her because he didn't want Betty to know how he felt about her. But his ex-wife was so eager to have him back that a blind man could see it. He'd never made any secret of his feelings for Betty. What an irony, that his wife should come back now, of all times, when Dana might have had some little chance to win his heart. Betty had walked in and taken him over, without a struggle. She wondered if she could ever forget the look in Hank's dark eyes when he'd stared at his ex-wife with such pain and longing. He still loved her. It was impossible not to know it. He might have enjoyed sleeping with Dana, but even so, he'd never shown any great desire to repeat the experience.

She put away the dishes and went to watch the evening news. Her father had liked this time of the day, when he was through with work, when they'd had a nice meal and he could sit with his coffee and listen to the news. He and Dana would discuss the day's events and then turn off the television and read. She'd missed that at Hank's elegant house. It was empty and cold. The television was in his study, not in the living room, and she'd never felt comfortable trespassing in there to watch it. She had none of her own favorite books, and his were all about horses and livestock and genetics. He read biographies, too, and there were some hardcover bestsellers that looked as if they'd never been opened at all.

Hank didn't make time to read for pleasure, she supposed. Most of his material seemed to be business-related.

She curled up in her father's armchair with tears stinging her eyes. She hadn't given way to tears in all the time she'd been married, and she wasn't going to cave in now, either, but she felt entitled to express a little misery while there was no one to see her.

She dabbed at tears, wondering why Hank had tried to stop her from leaving since he'd said he didn't want her anymore. Maybe it was the thought of ending their brief marriage so soon. It would be hard on the pride of a man like that to have failed more than once as a husband.

After a while, she got up and turned on a movie. It was one she'd seen half a dozen times but she only wanted the noise for company. She had to consider what she was going to do for the rest of her life. At this point, she was certain that she couldn't go on trying to keep the wolf from the door while she fought to maintain the small cattle ranch. She didn't have the working capital, the proper facilities or the money to trade for more livestock. The best way to go would be to just sign the whole thing over to Hank before it bankrupted her, and use the trust fund her mother had given her to pay for a college education. With that, she could find a job and support herself. She wouldn't need help from anyone; least of all from a reluctant husband. There was no alimony in Texas, but Hank had a conscience and he'd want to provide for her after the divorce. She wanted to be able to tell him she didn't want it.

Her plans temporarily fixed in her mind, she turned her attention to the movie. It was nice to have things settled.

Hayden Grant didn't have anything settled, least of all his mind. He was on the way to Corpus Christi with Bob and Betty, only half listening to the radio as he followed behind the couple, they in their Mercedes, he in his Lincoln.

He could have gone in the car with them; something he thought Betty was secretly hoping for. But he wanted to be alone. His ex-wife had fouled everything up with her untimely reappearance. Her taunts had caused him to be cruel to Dana, who'd had nothing from him except pain. He'd forced her into marriage whether she wanted it or not, seduced her in a fever of desire, and then brought her home and literally ignored her for two weeks. Looking back, he couldn't explain his own irrational behavior.

Since the night he'd been with Dana, his only thought had been of how sweet it was to make love to her. He hadn't dreamed that he could want anyone so much. But his feelings had frightened him because they were so intense, and he'd withdrawn from her. Betty's intervention had been the coup de grace, putting a wall between himself and Dana.

But desire wasn't the only thing he felt for his young wife, and for the first time he had to admit it. He remembered Dana at the age of sixteen, cuddling a wounded puppy that some cruel boy had shot with a rifle and crying with anger as she insisted that Hank drive her to the vet's. The puppy had died, and Hank had comforted the young girl whose heart sounded as if it might break. Dana had always been like that about little, helpless things. Her heart embraced the whole world. How could he have hurt her so, a woman like that?

He groaned out loud. He wondered if he'd lost his reason with Betty's return. He'd dreaded it because he thought he was still in love with Betty. He wasn't. He knew it quite suddenly when he saw Dana with tears in her eyes and her suitcase in her hand. Dana had lived with him for two weeks, and he hadn't even touched her since their wedding night. He thought of it with incredulity. Now he realized what his behavior had masked. He'd been afraid of falling so deeply in love with her that it would be as it had been with Betty. Except that Dana wasn't mercenary. She wanted him, and seemed to be ashamed of feeling that way. But she had a tender heart, and she'd cared about him. If he'd tried, he might have made her love him. The thought, once dreaded, was now the essence of heaven.

It was too late, though. He'd let her leave and he wouldn't be able to get her back. He'd lost her. What the hell was he doing driving to Corpus Christi with two people he didn't even like?

As he thought it, he realized that they were already driving into its city limits. It was too late to turn back now. He'd do what he'd promised, he thought, but after that, he was going home to Dana. Whatever it took, he was going to get her back.

If only it had been that easy. They'd no sooner gotten out of the car at the Collins's white brick mansion when Bob groaned and then fell. He died right there on the green lawn before the ambulance could get to him, despite Hank's best efforts to revive him. He'd had another stroke.

Betty went to pieces and Hank found himself in the ironic position of arranging a funeral for his ex-wife's second husband; and his former friend.

Back home, Dana heard about Bob Collins's death; it was all over the radio. He'd been a prominent man in the state's poultry industry and was well-known and liked. His funeral was very big and many important people attended it. Dana saw newspaper clippings of Hank supporting the grieving widow. She couldn't imagine that cold-eyed woman grieving for her husband. If Betty was crying, it was because Bob's life insurance policy had probably lapsed.

Dana chided herself for her uncharitable thoughts and threw the newspaper into the trash. Well, one thing was certain, Hayden Grant would be asking for a divorce so that he could remarry the woman he really loved. If Betty was what he wanted, he should have her. Dana remembered what she'd said to Bob Collins about not wanting to eat her heart out for the rest of her life with a man who wanted someone else. Poor Bob, who'd done exactly that, steadfastly, for ten long years. Dana offered a silent prayer for him. At least now perhaps he would have peace.

Two long weeks passed, with no word from Hank. The next morning, Dana went to see the family lawyer and asked him to initiate divorce proceedings. It would mean dipping into her small trust fund to pay for it, but that didn't matter. She wanted Hank to be happy.

"This isn't wise," the attorney tried to advise her. "You've been upset and so has he. You should wait, think it over."

She shook her head. "I've done all the thinking I care to. I want the deeds made up for my signature and delivered to Hank, along with the divorce papers. I'm throwing in the towel. Betty's free now and Hank deserves a little happiness. God knows he's waited long enough to get her back."

The attorney winced as he looked at the vulnerable, pale woman sitting in front of him. She'd suffered, judging by the thinness of her face and those terrible shadowed blue eyes. He couldn't imagine a man crazy enough to turn down a love that violent and selfless. But if she was right, that's exactly what Hayden Grant had already done. He sighed inwardly. Talk about throwing gold away in favor of gloss! Some men just didn't know their luck.

"I'll have everything ready by tomorrow morning. You're absolutely sure?"

She nodded.

"Then consider it done."

She thanked him and went home. The house was very empty and she felt the same. There would be a new life ahead of her. She was closing a very firm door on the old one, starting tomorrow. That thought was fixed firmly in her mind until the morning came and she began to throw up as if she were dying. She made it to the attorney's office to sign the papers, but she was too sick to travel.

Fearful that she had some virus that would prevent her plans to move, she made an appointment to see Dr. Lou Coltrain, a newly married member of the local medical community.

Lou examined her, asked pertinent questions and began to whistle softly while Dana looked at her with horror.

"It must have been some wedding night," Lou said, tongue in cheek, "because you've only been married a month and I know Hayden Grant. He wouldn't have touched you until the ring was in place."

"Lou, you're awful!" Dana groaned, flushing.

"Well, I'm right, too." She patted the younger woman on the shoulder. "It's two weeks too early for tests to tell us anything positive. Come back then. But meanwhile, you watch what medications you take and get plenty of rest, because I've seen too many pregnancies to mistake one. Congratulations."

"Thanks. But you, uh, won't tell anyone, right?" Dana asked gently.

"Your secret is safe with me." The doctor chuckled. "Want to surprise him, I guess?"

"That's right," Dana said immediately, thinking what a surprise it would have been.

"Come back and see me in two weeks," Lou repeated, "and I'll send you to Jack Howard up in Victoria. He's the best obstetrician I know, and it's a lot closer than Houston."

"Thanks, Lou."

"Anytime."

Dana went home in a cloud of fear and apprehension and joy. She was almost certainly pregnant, and her marriage was in tatters. But she knew what she was going to do. First she had to find her way to Houston, get an apartment and find a job. She'd handed the deeds to her father's property and the divorce petition over to the attorney for disposition. Presumably, he'd have already forwarded them to Hank in Corpus Christi in care of the bereaved Mrs. Collins. She'd burned her bridges and there was no going back.

Unaware of what was going on in Corpus Christi, Dana set out for Houston the next morning, painfully working out a future without Hank while a tall man with shocked dark eyes was served a divorce petition and ~ursed her until he went hoarse.

Hank jerked up the phone, oblivious to Betty's shocked stare, and dialed the phone number of the attorney, who vas also a friend of his.

"Luke, what the hell's going on?" he demanded, shaking the divorce papers at the receiver. "I didn't ask her for the deeds to the ranch, and I sure as hell don't remember asking for a divorce!"

"There, there, old fellow, calm down," Luke said firmly. "She said it was the best thing for both of you. Besides, you're going back to Betty anyway."

"I am?" he asked, shocked.

"That's what Dana told me. See here, Hank, you're throwing over a good woman. She never thought of herself once. It was what you wanted, what you needed to make you happy that she considered when she arranged all this. She said it would give you a head start on all the happiness you'd missed out on ten years ago, and she was glad for you."

"Glad for me." He looked at the papers and glanced irritably at Betty, who'd been practicing bereavement for two weeks while trying to entangle Hank in her web again. She hadn't succeeded. He was untangling Bob's finances for her, and they were in one major mess. It had taken time he didn't want to spend here, but for Bob's sake he'd managed it. Now he only wanted to go home and reclaim his wife, but he was holding proof that she didn't want to be reclaimed.

"She knew you'd be happy to have the matter dealt with before you came back," he continued. "Listen, if you don't contest the divorce—and why should you, right?—I can get it through in no time."

Hank hesitated, breathing deliberately so that he wouldn't start swearing at the top of his lungs. The words on the pages blurred in his sight as he remembered the last time he'd seen Dana. He mentally replayed the cruel, hateful things he'd said to her. No wonder she was divorcing him. She didn't know how he felt; he'd never told her. She thought he hated her. What a laugh!

"Can you hold it back for a few weeks?" he asked the attorney. "I've got some things to untangle down here for Bob's widow, and I can't get back home for a week, possibly longer."

"I can, but she won't like it," Luke said.

"Don't tell her."

"Hank..."

"Don't tell her," he repeated. "Leave it alone until I get back."

There was a heavy sigh. "If she asks me, point-blank, I won't lie to her."

"Then make sure she doesn't have the opportunity to ask you."

"I'll try."

"Thanks."

He hung up. He felt sick. God, what a mess he'd made of his life!

Betty sidled close and leaned against his arm, wearing a wispy negligee. "Poor old dear, is she leaving you?" she asked softly. "I'm sorry. Why don't you come upstairs with me and I'll kiss you better?"

He looked at her as if he hadn't heard correctly. "Betty, your husband was buried week before last," he said.

She shrugged. "He'd run out of money and he was barely able to get around by himself." She smiled in a shallow, childlike way, and he realized that she was just that—childlike. She had no depth of emotion at all, just a set of wants and needs that she satisfied the best she knew how, with her body. He'd lived with her for two years, ached for her for ten more, and he'd never known the sort of person she really was until he became involved with Dana. Now he could see the real difference between the two women.

He removed her hand from his arm. "I have some things to finish," he told her. "We'll talk later. Okay?"

She smiled. "Okay, lover."

CHAPTER SIX

IT TOOK ALL OF ANOTHER ten days for Hayden to wrap up the odds and ends of Bob's life and get his affairs safely into the hands of a good local attorney. Bob had an attorney, but the man had been evasive and almost impossible to locate. Finally it had taken the threat of litigation to get him to turn over needed documents. And afterward, the man—who had a degree in law from an interesting but unaccredited law school overseas—had vanished. It was no wonder that Bob had lost most of his money. The charlatan had embezzled it. Fortunately there would be enough left, added to the life insurance, to keep Betty fairly secure if she was careful.

It was only as he explained things to her and she realized that he wasn't going to propose marriage that she came apart for real.

"But you love me," she exclaimed. "You always have. Look at how quickly you married that child just so I wouldn't think you were carrying a torch for me!"

"It might have started that way," he replied quietly. "It didn't end that way. I can't afford to lose her now."

"Oh, she's got money, I guess."

He frowned. "No. She hasn't a dime in the world. Do you always ascribe mercenary reasons to every decision?"

"Of course I do," she said, and smiled faintly. "Security is the most important thing in the world. I didn't have anything when I was a child. I went hungry sometimes. I promised myself it would never happen to me." She made an awkward gesture with her shoulder. "That's

70

why I left you, you know. You were heading into debt and I was scared. I did love you, in my way, but there was Bob and he had a lot of money and he wanted me." She smiled. "I had no choice, really."

"I don't suppose you did." He was remembering that Dana had nothing, and she was giving him the only thing of worth in her possession, those deeds to the land, so that he wouldn't face the threat of some dangerously noisy neighbor. He could have kicked himself for letting her walk out of the house in the first place.

"I felt sort of sorry for her," she added thoughtfully. "She isn't sophisticated, is she? She was afraid of me." Her eyebrows met. "Why won't you sleep with her?"

He averted her eyes. "That's none of your business."

"It is, in a way. You won't sleep with me, either. Why?"

He grimaced. "I don't want you," he admitted reluctantly. "I'm sorry."

"You used to," she recalled. "You wanted me all the time. I thought it was going to kill you when I walked out."

"It damned near did. But things have changed." His eyes were sad and quiet. "I am sorry, Betty. For your loss, for everything."

"Bob wasn't a bad man," she said. "I was fond of him. I guess I'll miss him, in a way." She looked up. "You're sure about not wanting me?"

He nodded.

She sighed and smiled again. "Well, that's that. At least I'll have enough money to make ends meet, thanks to you. And I'm still young enough to make a good third marriage!"

On that note, he said his goodbyes and went back to the motel where he'd been staying. It felt nice to have the weight of Betty's disastrous finances off his shoulders, although he'd enjoyed untangling the mess.

Now he was going to go home and work on his own problems.

He looked at the divorce petition and the deeds and his eyes narrowed. Dana had wasted no time at all turning over the ranch to him. He began to frown. Where was she going to live without her house?

He picked up the phone and dialed the attorney's number, but he was told that Luke was in court on a case and couldn't be reached. Really worried now, he dialed the Mobry ranch number. It rang twice and the line was connected. He started to speak. Just as he did, a mechanical voice informed him that the number had been disconnected.

Frustrated and worried, his next call was to his own house, where he found Tilly.

"All right, what the hell's going on? Where did Dana go?" he demanded without preamble.

"She wouldn't let me call you," Tilly said stiffly. "I begged, but she wouldn't budge. I gave my word. Couldn't break it."

"Where is she?"

"She's left," came the terse reply. "Said you had the deeds and that Joe and Ernie would keep watch over the place until you made other arrangements, but you'd have to pay them."

"Oh, to hell with the ranch!" he snapped. "Where is she?"

"Took a cab to the bus station. Got the bus to Houston. I don't know where she went from there."

Hope raised its head. "Houston! Tilly, you're a wonder!"

"There's, uh, something else. The nurse who works for Dr. Lou Coltrain is a cousin of mine. Seems Dana went to see Lou before she left town. If you don't find her pretty soon, you're going to be looking for two people instead of one," she said, and hung up.

He stared at the telephone blankly and felt all the blood draining out of his face. Dana was pregnant? He counted back to their wedding night and realized that neither of them had even thought about precautions. His Dana was going to have a baby, and she'd left him! What an idiot he'd been!

He called the airport. Houston was a good place to start, thanks to Tilly, who'd saved him hours of tracking. But it was a big city, and he didn't even know where to start. He cursed himself for every painful thing he'd ever said to her. It couldn't be too late to convince her how much he cared, it just couldn't!

He soon realized how impossible it was going to be to locate Dana in Houston. She had a little money, but it would soon run out if she didn't get a job. He had to find her quickly, so he went straight to one of the better-known Houston detectives, and told him everything he knew about Dana including a description.

"Do you have a photo of your wife, Mr. Grant?" Dane Lassiter asked the man across the desk from him. A former Texas Ranger, Dane had built his agency from scratch, and now it had a fine national reputation for doing the impossible.

The question startled Hank, who hadn't expected it. He looked uncomfortable. "No," he said.

The other man didn't comment, but his eyes were steady and curious. No wonder, because the table behind Lassiter's desk carried a family photo of the detective, his attractive wife and two young sons who looked just like him.

"We're newlyweds," Hayden felt constrained to explain. "It was a quick marriage."

Dane didn't say a word. He was busy writing things down. "Did she run away, Mr. Grant?" he asked suddenly, and his black eyes pinned the other man.

Hayden took a sharp, angry breath. "Yes," he said through his teeth. "I did something stupid and I deserve to lose her. But I don't think I can stand to, just the same." He leaned forward and rested his forearms on his splayed legs in a defeated position. "And she's pregnant," he added through his teeth.

Hank's predicament sounded very familiar to Dane Lassiter. He knew all about pregnant women who ran away.

"We'll find her," Dane told the man, not so distant now. "You've given us some good leads, we'll check them out. Where can I reach you?"

Hayden gave the name of a local hotel. "I'll be here until I hear from you," he added, and he had the look of a man who planned to stay there until the turn of the century if that's how long it took.

"Okay. I'll get right on it." He stood up and shook hands. "Women need a lot of tenderness. They get hurt easily, and they keep secrets," he said surprisingly. "But if it helps, you learn how to cope with it after a while."

Hayden smiled. "Thanks."

Dane shrugged. He smiled back. "I've been married a long time. Nobody starts out in paradise. You sort of have to work up to it."

"I'll remember that. I hope I get the chance to find out firsthand."

It took two days for Dane to track Dana to a small boarding house outside Houston. During that time, Hayden lost sleep and thought torturously of all the things that could have happened to his errant, pregnant wife. It didn't improve his temper, or his heartache.

When Dane called, he was over the moon. He wasted no time at all getting to Mrs. Harper's Boarding House, but when he pulled up at the front steps in the Lincoln he'd rented at the airport on his arrival in Houston, he didn't know quite what to say. He stared at the big white house with longing and apprehension. His wife was in there, but she didn't want him. She'd tried to divorce him, had moved here and she'd made a good effort to erase her presence from his life. She hadn't even said a word to him about her pregnancy. How did he talk to her, what did he say to cancel out all the hurts he'd dealt her?

He got out of the car and approached the house slowly. His steps dragged, because he dreaded what was coming. He went up and rang the doorbell. A plump, smiling elderly woman opened the door.

"May I help you?" she asked politely.

"I'm Hayden Grant," he said in a subdued tone. "My wife lives here, I believe. Her name is Dana."

"Miss Mobry is your wife?" she asked, puzzled. "But I'm sure she said she wasn't married."

"She's very much married," he replied. He removed his cream-colored Stetson, belatedly, and let the hand holding it drop to his side. "I'd like to see her."

She gnawed on her lip, frowning. "Well, she's not here at the moment," she said. "She went to see that new adventure movie playing at the shopping center. With Mr. Coleman, that is."

He looked vaguely homicidal. "Who's Mr. Coleman?" he asked shortly.

"He lives here, too," she stammered, made nervous by the black glitter of his eyes. "He's a very nice young man . . ."

"Which shopping center and which movie?" he demanded.

She told him. She didn't dare not to.

He stomped back to his car, slammed into it and skidded on his way out the driveway.

"Oh, dear, oh, dear," Mrs. Harper mumbled. "I wonder if I shouldn't have mentioned that David is eleven years old..."

Sadly unaware of the age of Dana's "date," Hank drove to the shopping center, parked the car and went straight to the theater. As luck would have it, the feature was just ending, so people were pouring out of three exits. He stood, glaring, until he spotted Dana.

She was talking to a small boy in a baseball cap, her face animated, smiling. His heart jumped as he watched her come out of the big building. He loved her. He hadn't known. He honestly hadn't known. His heart accelerated wildly, but his eyes began to glow from within, quiet and watchful and adoring.

Dana was too far away to see his expression. But she spotted him at once and stopped dead in her tracks. The boy was saying something, but she wasn't listening. Her face was stark white.

Hank approached her, alert to any sudden movement. If she tried to run, he'd have her before she got three steps.

But she didn't run. She lifted her chin as if in preparation for battle and her hands clenched the small purse she was holding against the waist of her denim skirt.

"Hello, Dana," he said when he was within earshot.

She looked at him warily. "How did you find me?" she asked.

"I didn't. A detective agency did."

She looked paler. "I signed all the necessary papers," she told him curtly. "You're free."

He stuck his hands deep into his pockets. "Am I?"

Dana turned to David and handed him a five-dollar bill. "Why don't you go back in there and play the arcade machine for a minute or two while I speak to this man, David?" she asked.

He grinned. "Sure, Miss Mobry, thanks!"

He was off at a lope.

"So you came with the boy, not with some other man," Hank murmured absently.

She flushed. "As if I'd trust my own judgment about men ever again! David's mother is at work, so I offered to treat him to a movie."

"You do like kids, don't you?" he asked, and his eyes were very soft as they fell to her waistline. "That's fortunate."

"That isn't what I'd call it," she said stubbornly.

He sighed. He didn't know what to say, but this certainly wasn't the ideal place to talk. "Look, suppose you go fetch the boy and we'll go back to your boarding house? Did you drive here?"

She shook her head. "We got a city bus." She wanted to argue, but he looked as if he was going to dig his heels in. She couldn't understand why he was here, when Betty was free. Perhaps that's what he wanted to explain. She seemed to have no choice but to do as he said, for the time being, at least.

"A city bus!" he muttered, and in her condition! But he didn't dare mention that he knew about her pregnancy. Not yet. "Get the boy," he said shortly. "I'll take you home."

She went to find David, and Hank drove them back to the boarding house. David thanked her and deserted her. Mrs. Harper hovered, but a hard glare from Hank dispatched her soon enough. He closed the door behind her and sat down in the one chair in Dana's room, while she perched on the bed a little nervously.

"Where's Betty?" she wanted to know.

"In Corpus Christi, I guess," he said. "I'm alone."

"You won't be alone for long," she reminded him. "You're getting married again."

"I'm already married," he said quietly. "I have a young and very pretty wife."

She flushed. "I divorced you."

He shook his head. "I stopped it."

"Why?" she asked miserably, her eyes eloquent in a face like rice paper. "You don't have to stay married to me now that she's free!"

He winced. He reached over and touched her cheek, but she jerked away from him.

He averted his face and stared down at the floor. "I don't want to remarry Betty."

She stared at his averted features, unconvinced. "You've never gotten over her, Hank," she said sadly. "You said yourself that part of the reason you married me was so she wouldn't know how you'd grieved since she divorced you."

"Maybe it was the old story of wanting what I couldn't have, or the grass being greener on the other side of the fence," he ventured.

She drew in a long breath. "Or maybe it was just that you never stopped loving her," she added, and the eyes that searched his were wistful and sad. "Oh, Hank, we can't love to order. We have to settle for what we can have in this life." Her eyes went to the floor. "I'll go back to school and work toward my degree and I'll be happy."

His eyes slid up to hers. "Without me?" he asked bluntly.

She wasn't sure how much he knew. She blinked and gathered her scattered wits. "Doesn't Betty want to marry you?" she asked suspiciously.

"More than ever," he affirmed.

"Then what's the problem?"

"I told you. The problem is that I don't want to marry her."

"I don't understand," she said uneasily.

He smiled wistfully. "I used to envy other men taking their sons on camping and fishing trips with them. I never thought I might have one of my own. But a girl would be nice, too. I guess girls can fish and hunt as well as boys can, if they're so inclined." His eyes lifted to hers. "You like to shoot, as I recall."

"I don't like to hunt," she replied, uneasy at the way he was talking about kids. He couldn't possibly *know*...

He shrugged. "I'll teach you to shoot skeet."

"Okay, but I won't cook them."

He chuckled. "Concrete won't tenderize."

"I know what a skeet target is made of." She drew in another breath. The way he was touching her made her toes tingle. "Betty might change her mind about having a child."

He shook his head. "And even if she did, she wouldn't want it, or love it. You will. You'll want our kids and spoil them rotten if I don't watch out." His eyes lifted. "Tilly's already looking forward to it. She's bought a food processor so she can make fresh baby food for him."

She flushed. "She's jumping the gun."

"No, she isn't," he said with a grin. "Tilly's kin to Dr. Lou Coltrain's office nurse."

"Oh, my God!" she said in a burst.

He shrugged. "So I know. The world won't end because you didn't tell me." His eyes darkened. "I'm sorry that I made it so rough on you that you didn't feel you could tell me."

She glared at him. "I'm not going back."

His shoulders seemed to fall. "I know I've made a lot of mistakes," he said. "You have to make allowances. Until a couple of weeks ago, I thought I was still in love with my ex-wife. I had to get to know her again to realize that she was an illusion. The reality of Betty was pretty harsh, after you."

"I don't understand."

"Don't you?" He sighed. "Well, Dana, I suppose I made an idol of her after she left. The one that got away is always better than anything that's left."

"You didn't act like someone who wasn't in love with his ex-wife," she reminded him as all the painful things he'd said to her returned in a flash of anger.

"All it took was two weeks in Corpus Christi to cure me," he returned. He leaned forward with his forearms resting on his knees and stared at the floor. "She's shallow," he said, glancing at Dana. "Shallow and selfish and spoiled. And I'd been away from her so long that I forgot. It cut the heart out of me when I realized that you went away because you thought I wanted Betty instead of you. I'm sorry for that."

"You can't help wanting someone else..."

"I want you, Dana," he said with a quizzical smile.

She clasped her hands hard at her waist. "You're just making the best of it, aren't you? You know about the baby and how I feel about you and you're sorry for me."

His heart jumped. "How you feel?" he prompted.

"You know that I'm in love with you," she said, avoiding his penetrating gaze. "That I have been since I was seventeen."

His heart wasn't jumping anymore, it had stopped. He barely could breathe. He certainly was robbed of speech.

She jerked one shoulder as she assumed his silence was one of regret for her sake, because he had nothing to give her. "Shameful, isn't it? I was still a kid. I couldn't even let boys kiss me, because I kept thinking about you. I've lived like a nun all these years, waiting and hoping, and it has to happen like this...you have to be forced into marriage just when your ex-wife is free again."

He hadn't known that she loved him. He'd known she wanted him, which was a very different thing altogether. He was stunned for a moment, and then overwhelmed, overjoyed.

"I'm sorry," she said on a long breath. "I guess we're both trapped."

"You'll need some maternity clothes," he remarked, clearing his throat. "Things to wear when we give parties. After all, I'm a rich man. We wouldn't want people to think I couldn't afford to dress you properly, would we?"

She frowned. "I'm not coming back..."

"We can turn that third guest room into a nursery," he continued, as if she hadn't spoken. "It's next door to the master bedroom, and we can leave the door open at night. I'll get a monitor, too," he added thoughtfully. "So if the baby has any problems at night, it will set off an alarm next to our bed. Or we could get a nurse for the first month or two. Would you like that?"

He'd made her speechless with plans. "I haven't thought about any of that," she stammered.

"Don't you want a settled life for our baby, with a mother and father who love him?" he persisted.

He cut the ground right out from under her with that last question. What could she say? Of course, she wanted a settled life for their child. But if Hank still loved Betty, what kind of life would it be?

Her eyes mirrored all her worries. He touched her cheek, and then smoothed back her disheveled hair. "I was trying to live in the past because I didn't have much of a present, or a future, unless you count making money. That's no longer true. I have something to look forward to now, something to challenge me, keep me going." He smiled. "I guess Tilly will make me miserable for a week, paying me back for the way I treated you. I won't be allowed to forget one rotten thing I said to you, and she'll burn the banana pudding every time

I ask her to make it.'' He sighed. ''But it will be worth it, if you'll just come home, Dana. Tilly's all aglow at the thought of having a baby in the house.''

''We've already discussed this,'' she began.

He bent and drew his lips tenderly across hers. ''Not really,'' he murmured. ''Open your lips a little, I can't taste you like this.''

''I don't wa...''

''Ummm, that's it,'' he whispered gently, and deepened the kiss.

She forgot what she was trying to think to say to him. Her arms curled up around his neck and she let him lift her over his legs, so that he could hold her gently across his body. He was gentle and slow, and very thorough. When he finally lifted his head, she couldn't think at all.

''I'm going to like being a father,'' he assured her. ''I won't mind sitting up with you when he's teething or giving bottles or changing diapers.''

''That's nice.''

He smiled. ''Do you have a lot to pack?''

''Just a few skirts and blouses and shoes. But I haven't said I'm going with you.''

''What's holding you back?'' he asked gently.

''You haven't explained why you don't want Betty back.''

''Oh. That.'' He shrugged. ''I don't love her. I'm not sure I ever did. I wanted her, but there's a big difference in lust and love.''

''Are you sure?''

''Considering the sort of man I am—and I think you know me pretty well by now—do you think I'm capable of making love to one woman when I'm in love with someone else?''

She searched his eyes. ''Well, no, I don't think so. You're pretty old-fashioned like that.''

He nodded. "So how could I have made love to you so completely that one time if I'd really been in love with Betty?"

"I'm sure most men wouldn't have refused something that was offered."

"We're talking about me. Would I?"

She grimaced. "No."

"That being the case, making love to you was something of a declaration of my feelings, wasn't it?"

It was. She caught her breath. "Oh, my goodness. I never considered that."

"Neither did I until I was well on my way to Corpus Christi," he admitted. "I called it guilt and remorse and misplaced emotion, I denied it to you and myself. But in the end, I came back because I loved you. And you weren't there." He smiled sadly. "I thought you'd fight Betty. I never expected you to run."

"I didn't think you wanted me. Women only fight when they know they're loved. I didn't." She searched his eyes, fascinated. "I don't guess you'd like to... say it?"

He grimaced. "Not really."

"Oh."

"But I could. If it matters that much." He looked down at her stomach. "I guess kids like to hear it, too, don't they?"

She nodded. "All the time."

He cleared his throat. "Okay. Give me a minute to get used to the idea."

She smiled with excitement and growing delight. "You can have as much as you need."

"Okay. I... love you."

Her eyebrows rose.

"I love you," he repeated, and this time it sounded as if he meant it. He stared down at her with wonder.

"By God, I do," he whispered huskily. "With all my heart, Dana, even if I didn't realize it."

She moved closer and slid her face into his hot throat, curling into him like a kitten. "I love you, too, Hank."

He smiled crookedly, staring past her head to the door. He hadn't expected it to be so easy to confess his deepest emotions. He'd never done it before, not even with Betty. His arms contracted. "I guess we're not the first people who ever fell in love."

"It feels like it, though, doesn't it?" she asked drowsily. "Oh, Hank, I wish my dad was still alive, so he'd know."

His hand smoothed over her hair. "He knows, Dana," he said at her temple, his voice deep and quiet and loving. "Somehow, I'm sure he knows."

She curled closer. "Perhaps he does."

CHAPTER SEVEN

THE BABY WAS BORN at two o'clock in the morning. Tilly sat in the emergency room cubicle in her robe and slippers, her hair in curlers, glaring at the disheveled man across from her who was sitting up, pale-faced, on the examination table thanking the doctor for his new son.

"It's a boy!" he exclaimed when the doctor moved out of sight. "And Dana's fine! I can see her as soon as they bring her out of the recovery room!"

"You saw her already," she muttered at him and cocked an eyebrow at his red face. "Just before you fainted..."

"I never!" he said. "I tripped over that gown they made me wear in the delivery room!"

"The one that only came to your knees?" she asked knowingly. "Dana was laughing so hard, she didn't even have to push. The baby just popped right out."

"I've had a hectic night," he began defensively.

"Sure, denying that it was labor pains, right up until her water broke. 'It's just false labor, sweetheart, you're only eight months and three weeks along,' you said. And there we were, rushing her to the hospital because you were afraid to wait for an ambulance, me in my nightgown, too! And then we no sooner get her into the delivery room when you see the baby coming out and faint dead away!"

He glared at her. "I didn't faint, I tripped...!"

She opened her mouth to argue just as a nurse peeked around the corner. "Mr. Grant, your wife is asking for you."

"I'll be right there."

"Are you feeling all right now?" she asked.

"I tripped," he said firmly.

The nurse and Tilly exchanged amused glances, but he didn't see them. "Yes, sir, I know you did, but we can't overlook any fall in a hospital."

"Sure. I knew that."

He followed the nurse down the hall until she stopped at a private room and stood aside to let him enter.

Dana was sitting up in bed with their son in her arms, tears of pure joy in her eyes as she watched the nurse stuff Hank into a gown and mask.

"Hospital rules," he muttered.

"Yes, sir, but all for baby's protection, and we know you don't mind," she replied with a grin.

He chuckled. "Of course not."

She tied the last tie and left him with his small family.

"Are you okay?" she asked.

He nodded. "Just a little shaky, and I did not faint," he added.

"Of course you didn't, darling," she agreed. "Come see what I've got."

She pulled back the flannel and exposed a perfect little boy. His eyes weren't even open just yet, and he looked tiny.

"He's going to grow, isn't he?" Hank asked worriedly.

"Of course he is!"

He touched the tiny head, fascinated. The baby was smaller than he'd expected, so fragile, so new. Tears stung his eyes as he looked at his very own son.

Seconds later, the tiny mouth opened and began to cry. Dana chuckled as she fumbled with the gown and got it off one shoulder, exposing a firm, swollen breast. While Hank watched, spellbound, she guided the tiny mouth to a hard nipple and caught her breath as he began to suckle.

Flushed, she looked up to find an expression of pure wonder on her husband's face.

"I know we talked about bottle feeding," she began.

"Forget we said a word," he replied. He stood over her, his eyes so full of love that they sparkled with it. "I hope you can do that for a year or so, because I love watching it."

She laughed a little self-consciously. "I love feeling it," she confessed, stroking the tiny head. "Oh, Hank, we've got a baby," she breathed ecstatically. "A real, live, healthy little boy!"

He nodded. He was too choked for speech.

"I love you."

He took a steadying breath. "I love you, honey," he replied. His eyes searched hers hungrily. "With all my heart."

"My paper husband," she murmured.

"Remembering?" he teased. "Me, too. But I feel pretty flesh and blood right now."

"You look it, too." She drew him down and kissed him through the mask. "Have you forgotten what day it is?"

He frowned. "Well, in all the excitement . . ."

"It's your birthday!"

His eyebrows arched. "It is?"

"Yes, it is." She grinned at him. "Like your present?" she added, nodding toward the baby feeding at her breast.

"I love it," he returned. "Do I get one of these every year?" he teased.

"I won't make any promises, but we'll see."

"That's a deal."

Tilly joined them minutes later, still in her gown and robe with her hair in curlers.

"Good Lord, haven't you gone home yet?" Hank asked, aghast.

She gave him an amused grin. "How?"

"You could..." He pursed his lips. "No money for a cab, and you can't drive."

"Got it."

He looked sheepish. "I'll drive you home right now." He bent and kissed Dana and his child. "I'll be back as soon as I drop off Tilly. Anything you want me to bring you?"

She nodded. "Strawberry ice cream."

"I'll be back in a flash!"

And he was. For years afterward, the small hospital staff talked about the day young Donald Mandel Grant was born, when his proud dad satisfied Dana's craving for strawberry ice cream by having a truckload of the most expensive made delivered to the hospital. Dana said that it was a shame their baby was too young to enjoy it, but Hank promised that he wouldn't miss out. Hank had just purchased an ice cream company, and he was waiting for their son's first birthday party with pure glee!

Bride in Waiting
Margaret Way

Dear Reader,

It's with the greatest pleasure I join the renowned Diana Palmer in our two-story project, *Husbands on Horseback*. Diana is not only a fine writer but a true friend. I still thank her for her kindness and support.

Like Diana, I enjoy writing about the Big Sky Country, which in Australia is our legendary Outback. There, one is powerfully and richly aware of the wholeness, the openness and the immensity of a cloudless, blue silk sky that at night turns to an ineffably beautiful diamond dazzle. In such an environment is it any wonder the men of the Outback have that wonderfully exhilarating spirit of liberation? It is inherited from their pioneering forebears for whom the realization of a dream lay beyond the coastal plains and The Great Dividing Range to the ever-beckoning Wild Heart. Our heroes of the Outback continue to suffer incredible hardships in a harsh land that miraculously, after rain, delivers the biblical promise of a flowering desert. Then, too, they know the fierce joys of self-sufficiency, of being tested, of developing inner resources, the techniques of survival and the prime satisfaction of wresting a living from a formidable earth. In *isolation*.

The man of the Outback is adventurous, enterprising, direct. He has humor—often dry—a stoic patience, a common-sense practicality and, above all, a distinctive sense of mateship that has come to define Australians. His natural style is magnificently sitting a horse. He even looks good slouching nonchalantly beside it. Something entirely fitting. I like to think my heroes grow out of the Big Sky Country itself. A unique environment that paradoxically magnifies—not diminishes—man.

I hope you enjoy the stories Diana and I offer.

Margaret Way

CHAPTER ONE

AS SHE got closer to Courtland Downs Carrie opened up the engine. The Jeep swept through miles of lush, open pastures, blue and green couch grass, para grass and spear grass on which herds of Brahman cattle with their floppy ears, prominent dewlaps and humped backs grazed peacefully alongside the prolific bird life. It was impossible to count the birds. Trillions of them! Swans, pelicans, ducks, geese, the jabirus on their tall, stick-like legs and the blue cranes, the famous dancing brolgas of the North. It was enough to enjoy them as people had enjoyed them from the beginning of time.

A curiously brassy sun, an effect of Cyclone Anita, standing stationary out to sea, threw rings of gold onto the deep green lagoons that were filled with abundant fish. Many a time Blake had sent over a haul of the magnificent eating fish, the barramundi, because he knew how much her mother had enjoyed them. Her mother had doted on Blake Courtland, which had to be the reason he continued to keep so much in touch.

As always when she thought of her mother, Carrie made a valiant effort to throw off the cloud of grief that descended on her.

Four years since her mother had died. Four years was a long and lonely time. A time of helpless, hopeless pining for a beloved face, a sweet voice. So many cries of the heart that were silent! She and her father never spoke about her mother at all. It was as if she had left them and they couldn't bear to speak of their loss. At twenty-three Carrie was expected to live with her sadness

and get on with her life. Her father, a Vietnam veteran,
had struck a critical decade of life. At fifty-two he had
sunk into deep depression. Carrie did her best, but she
could never replace her mother. Neither did she have her
mother's unique gift for easing her father out of his black
moods. At least her twin brothers, Sean and Steven, had
one another and a career ahead of them in medicine.

Losses. Losses. Losses, Carrie thought, staring toward
the horizon, her delicate jaw tight. It took moments more
for the pain in her throat to subside. Everything was fine
as long as she kept herself busy.

The hills in the distance were a radiant amethyst, three
spurs of the Great Dividing Range, which formed a
semicircle to enclose this wonderful natural catchment
area that was Courtland Downs. She never approached
the station without a strange feeling of homecoming.
There was such a compelling sense of peace, of space,
of *nature.* Even the cattle looked perfect, as well they
might. Courtland Downs was one of the finest cattle-
breeding establishments in the country, and the an-
cestral home of the clan.

Carrie glanced at her watch. Two-thirty. She prayed
Blake would be at home. At least she knew he was in
residence. Everyone in the district liked to keep track of
Blake's movements, whether he was in the state capital
or on one of his overseas business trips. Blake Courtland
was the most powerful and glamorous man in their part
of the world. "A god of the rainforest," as one of her
girlfriends had fancifully called him.

The Jeep bounced over a stone bridge, and Carrie accelerated in preparation for the steep climb. The avenue
of magnificent Cuban royals was just ahead, fronds
waving in the strong blow that again signalled a cyclone
was in range of the coast. The towering palms led the
eye past acres of beautiful tropical gardens to the col-
onial mansion that stood serenely atop the hill. It com-

manded spectacular views of the hinterland and out over the sapphire blue sea and offshore islands. The setting was breathtaking, *unique*. There were some sights a person could never forget.

The Courtlands were the elite, the serious rich. It was a good thing they gave so much away, Carrie thought wryly. Courtland money went to hospitals, charities, medical research and youth foundations. In the past year Blake had built a state-of-the-art sports complex for the young people of the district, who quite frankly idolized him. If the people of the North were asked to elect a president of a future republic, Carrie was sure Blake's name would be high on the list.

Yet Blake had suffered his own tragedies. His father, Sir Talbot Courtland, had been killed in a light plane crash while holidaying in New Zealand's mountainous South Island. Blake's beautiful and much admired fiancée, Amanda Anthony, an experienced equestrienne, had taken a fatal fall in a cross-country event some years before. Carrie couldn't bear to ponder the pain Blake must have suffered. She'd been eighteen at the time, in her first year at University in Brisbane. Her mother had rung her with the tragic news. Sudden death was a fact of life and the cause of many a terrible crisis for those who had to go on alone. Blake was as vulnerable as anyone else, but he had enormous reserves of inner strength. She wished she didn't have to trouble him now, but there was little alternative, not when her father seemed to have lost all heart.

Carrie brought the Jeep to a halt just outside the massive electronically controlled gates that proved a marvellous entry to the estate. One of the groundsmen taking his turn on the gate threw the switch that operated the hydraulic arm system.

"Hi there, Miss Donovan!" He saluted her. "Go right up."

Carrie returned the cheerful smile, thinking with some surprise she had to be on a list that said Admit, No Questions Asked.

A fountain graced the circular driveway, and as she swung to the left she saw several cars parked in the roseate shade of the blossoming poincianas.

Why hadn't she stopped to think he might have visitors? Surely that was the mayor's car? There could be an important meeting in progress, something to do with emergency management should the cyclone hit. She would just have to wait.

Carrie got out of the vehicle, smoothing the folds of her blue skirt. She wasn't looking her best, she knew, but *presentable*. She was still wearing the pink tank top she had put on that morning, but she had changed her jeans and slipped sandals on her feet. At least she had tamed the masses of her hair, gathering it into a single thick braid. She was too tall and too thin. She didn't see she was immensely graceful.

Carrie walked up the short flight of steps and onto the wide veranda. The tall double doors were open, giving her a clear view of the hallway and the wonderful antique chandelier. The gleaming parquet floor, the rosy glow of a Persian rug, the circular library table that held a very beautiful arrangement of orchids, lilies and big glossy leaves. A series of graceful arches on either side of the hallway led to the formal rooms.

Not the home for ordinary folk. A house for multimillionaires. What did it feel like to have all that money? she wondered. To her and her father, beset by financial worries, it was mind-boggling.

Carrie pressed the door chimes, expecting one of the staff to appear, but Blake himself came to the door, the jewel-eyed gaze that never failed to startle her undergoing some subtle change when he saw her.

PLAY
HARLEQUIN'S

LUCKY HEARTS
GAME

AND YOU GET

- ★ **FREE BOOKS**
- ★ **A FREE GIFT**
- ★ **AND MUCH MORE**

**TURN THE PAGE AND
DEAL YOURSELF IN** ➔

PLAY "LUCKY HEARTS" AND YOU GET . . .

★ **Exciting Harlequin Romance® novels—FREE**

★ **PLUS a Beautiful Porcelain Trinket Box—FREE**

THEN CONTINUE YOUR LUCKY STREAK WITH A SWEETHEART OF A DEAL

1. Play Lucky Hearts as instructed on the opposite page.

2. Send back this card and you'll receive brand-new Harlequin Romance® novels. These books have a cover price of $3.75 each, but they are yours to keep absolutely free.

3. There's no catch. You're under no obligation to buy anything. We charge nothing — ZERO — for your first shipment. And you don't have to make any minimum number of purchases — not even one!

4. The fact is thousands of readers enjoy receiving books by mail from the Harlequin Reader Service. They like the convenience of home delivery…they like getting the best new novels month before they're available in stores…and they love our discount prices!

5. We hope that after receiving your free books you'll want to remain a subscriber. But the choice is yours — to continue or cancel, anytime at all! So why not take us up on our invitation, with no risk of any kind. You'll be glad you did!

THE HARLEQUIN READER SERVICE®: HERE'S HOW IT WORKS

Accepting free books places you under no obligation to buy anything. You may keep the books and gift and return the shipping statement marked "cancel". If you do not cancel, about a month later we'll send you 6 additional novels, and bill you just $3.10 each plus 25¢ delivery per book and GST.* That's the complete price–and compared to cover prices of $3.75 each–quite a bargain! You may cancel at any time, but if you choose to continue, every month we'll send you 6 more books, which you may either purchase at the discount price…or return to us and cancel your subscription.

*Terms and prices subject to change without notice.

Canadian residents will be charged applicable provincial taxes and GST.

If offer card is missing, write to: Harlequin Reader Service, P.O. Box 609, Fort Erie, Ontario L2A 5X3

0195619199-L2A5X3-BR01

HARLEQUIN READER SERVICE
PO BOX 609
FORT ERIE ONT
L2A 9Z9

Canada Post Corporation/Société canadienne des postes
Postage paid   Port payé
If mailed in Canada   si posté au Canada

Business   **Réponse**
Reply   **d'affaires**

0195619199   01

MAIL▶POSTE

"Carolyn! What a surprise!" He didn't smile, and she was glad. His smile was too disturbing.

"I'm sorry, Blake." Her hand moved through a delicate arc. "I didn't stop to think you might have visitors. That the mayor's car, isn't it?"

He glanced beyond her. Tall, rangy, splendid, fine-boned head, a sheen on his blue-black hair and sun-coppered skin. "It is, but we've nearly finished our meeting. Come in, Carolyn. If you don't mind waiting in my study, I shouldn't be long." His gaze returned to her. Blue. So very, very blue. Like the deep sparkling waters off the reef. Being hypnotised must be like this, she thought. All that stupendous power in one pair of eyes. She stood for a moment, trying to control the treacherous upsurge of unwanted emotion.

She had known Blake all her life, but these past few years had been different. Despite the polite amenities they usually indulged in, some deep silent current ran between them.

She knew it. So did he. Sometimes it frightened her.

"Carolyn?" he prompted.

Daydreams were dangerous. Didn't she know that by now? All thousand and one of them.

"Thank you, Blake. I won't take up too much of your valuable time."

He made a little scornful sound at the formality of her tone, taking her arm and drawing her over the threshold. A commanding man, who made a woman feel like a woman. His touch instantly caused spasms of sensation. A queer vertigo that almost made her dizzy. Whenever she was near him she felt this near panic, as though he was drawing closer and closer to the very heart of her. It was a risk she took every time they met.

They were barely at the first archway when a young woman emerged from the drawing room on the opposite side of the hallway. Her glowing expression altered radically when she saw Carrie.

"*You*, Carrie." She sounded mightily surprised.

Carrie scarcely noticed the ludicrous lack of warmth. She was too busy trying to control her own shock. Diane Anthony's resemblance to her late sister was startling. Something new had happened in the few months since Carrie had last seen her. Diane had had her trademark long blond hair cut. She now wore it in a medium pageboy with a full, shining fringe that drew attention to her large hazel eyes. It was a style that instantly conjured up sharp mental visions of Amanda.

Even after five years Carrie thought such a reminder would cause Blake more pain than pleasure. Surely Diane had considered that herself?

"Hello, Diane. How are you?" She sounded just about right. Pleasant. Casual.

"Fine. Fine." Diane was busy contemplating Carrie's hair, face and clothes. Not even her sandals were missed. "It's not often we see *you* here."

"Emergency," Carrie said.

"Why, it must be all of three months."

"The dinner-dance at the golf club," Carrie reminded her. "We'll have to wait for the next big occasion." It was wrong of her, but Carrie couldn't resist a little dig. Unlike her late sister, Diane Anthony didn't have a warm, friendly manner. She was distinctly stand-offish, with a great sense of her family's wealth. A few years older than Carrie, Diane had never made the slightest attempt to be friendly.

After such an exchange it wasn't surprising Blake decided to move off. "I'll be with you all in a moment, Di," he said briskly. "Keep everyone happy."

"No problem!" Another brilliant smile and a powerful message to Carrie that Diane was on her home ground

"Nice to see you, Carrie." She said it as though she couldn't care less.

"Bye." Carrie lifted a friendly hand. What else was here to do?

"Di's not as bad as she sometimes sounds," Blake offered dryly as they reached the study.

"You know her better than I do." Carrie's tone was mild.

He opened the door of the study, allowing her to precede him into the large, handsome room. "My theory is she sees you as some sort of threat."

Carrie spun around, her eyes the iridescent green of a butterfly's wing. "Good grief, in what way?"

"Competition, in a word. You have more than your share of admirers in the district. Tim McConnell among them. That didn't escape Di's attention at the dinner-dance."

Carrie looked sceptical. "You're not going to tell me she's in love with him?"

Blake shrugged. "I think it may be more she regards him as her property."

"Really?" Dryness crept into Carrie's attractive voice. "Then as the French say, stiff fromage." She made a little graceful turn going to an armchair and sitting down. "Please don't let me keep you, Blake. I'll sit quietly in this comfortable chair."

His blue eyes slid over her, taking in her extreme slenderness. "It pleases me to see you get *any* bit of rest."

"I'm not overworked," she protested.

"I think you are." His answer was equally crisp. "I expect you're worried about the harvest, as well?"

"Enough to come to you."

"Can you make that a little less hostile?"

Carrie flushed. "Forgive me, I'm not hostile at all. It's just that—"

"You don't like to bother me?"

She sighed. "You're absolutely right."

"Why not?"

Was he taunting her? "Are you serious now, or is this my day for being put in my place?"

"Carolyn," he drawled, "that would be quite a job. Under the politeness, you're my favorite little firecracker."

"Red hair can be a problem. I'm not so *little*, either."

"I don't know that I mind tall women." He picked up some papers on his desk, then turned to the door. "I'd better get back. We can continue this fascinating conversation later on. Have you had something to eat? You're as thin as a bird."

Carrie shook her head. "Look, I'm strong. That's important."

"Any thinner and you'd break. I'll arrange afternoon tea for you."

She stared at him, paying him back with a flippant remark. "No wonder everyone loves you."

"And you?" He turned so abruptly, it startled her.

"Sometimes," she admitted, off balance.

"And other times?"

"I refuse to be drawn."

"I think I could get it out of you if I had to." It was one of those days when the sonic signals were flashing back and forth. "My instinct says yes."

He laughed then, the very image of vibrant male power. "Give me fifteen minutes to see everyone off. Meanwhile you can take refuge in afternoon tea."

Left on her own, Carrie fingered a ridge of the expensive leather armchair. She felt just a little sick. Excitement did that to her. *Blake*. She began to breathe deeply, in and out. In and out. It wasn't often Blake went out of his way to unsettle her, but when he *did*!

She turned her attention deliberately to the large portrait of Sir Talbot Courtland that had pride of place above a mantelpiece flanked by splendid Georgian bookcases. What a fine-looking man he had been! A gentleman to his fingertips. Blake looked very much like his father, but he had his mother's astonishing sapphire blue eyes.

Who could ever have foreseen the tragedies that had befallen them all? Certainly not Lady Courtland, who had to be hospitalised for several days after her husband's crash. These days Lady Courtland lived in Sydney with her sister, visiting Blake several times a year. Blake had two sisters, as well, both married to influential men within Courtland Enterprises. One way and another, there was quite a Courtland clan. Since her mother had died and the twins had gone off to med school in Brisbane, there was only she and her father. And for how much longer she didn't know. Michael Donovan had survived a terrible war in Vietnam, but in the past few years he had devised his own strategy for killing himself.

Carrie closed her eyes sadly, picturing the events of the morning. Events that had left her distraught and desperately in need of Blake's help.

By five o'clock she was up and dressed and eating a light breakfast of tea and toast in the kitchen. She didn't sit down at the table but roamed restlessly around the room, half listening to the banter of the early morning radio announcer while she waited for the latest cyclone watch bulletin. Tropical Cyclone Anita, the first of the season, was causing concern all along the far northern seaboard. Classified by the bureau as a category two tropical cyclone with gusts up to a hundred and seventy kilometres an hour, it had the capacity to cause significant damage to property, trees, power lines and crops. Stationary now, all that could change. Cyclones were dangerous and unpredictable, as Carrie knew well. In

Australia they moved in far more erratic paths than in other parts of the world.

In their own district, the mango crop was almost but not quite ready for harvest, but no grower, including her father, would be prepared to leave the valuable crop on the trees if faced with possible torrential rain and gale force winds. Decisions would have to be made, and that in itself presented a problem. There were only so many pickers and packers to go round. Every plantation would begin harvesting as a matter of urgency when the usual production period was spread over six to eight weeks through early November to late December. The biggest plantations would get top priority. She had no quarrel with that, but they desperately needed a good year. For all the hard work, her father had made some bad decisions over the past few years. His increasingly heavy gambling didn't help, either. Carrie thought with anguish how Blake had opened his chequebook for her father on more than one occasion in recent times. He had to be paid back.

She sighed deeply, walked to the large square window over the kitchen sink and looked out. The birds were shrieking ecstatically, revelling in the light rain that was falling and the abundant nectar from all the blossoming trees. The branches fairly danced with lorikeets and parakeets, brilliant jewel flashes or the soft pinks and greys of the chattering galahs. How beautiful they were. How joyful.

She turned away abruptly, beset by worry. Her father hadn't come home last night. Another night of poker with a few of his ex-Army mates. All Vietnam veterans. Another night of heavy drinking. She'd long since stopped ringing around to check on his safety. He always found out, and it always made him angry. Carrie loved her father and was intensely loyal to him. She remembered the good times. Her childhood, when he had sung songs to them in his beautiful baritone voice, or made up stories. Such stories! Funny, curious and sometimes so downright scary they had to huddle up together in delicious fright. She and her adored little brothers, Sean and Steven, four years her junior and her little pals. Their father had taught them all how to swim, to ride, how to handle a boat and become expert anglers.

''Wild and handsome Mick Donovan,'' as he'd been known in his youth. He'd been little more than a boy when he'd gone off to Vietnam, thinking it was going to be an adventure. The adventure had altered him at once and forever.

Carrie resembled her father closely in looks. She had his thick flame mahogany hair, his dark green eyes, his distinctive black lashes and black winged brows. She even had his dimple in her chin, but where hers was delicate his was a deep cleft. The twins took after the Pagets, their mother's side of the family. Quiet, classic good looks, fair hair and grey eyes. Her father had always said their mother had been psychologically oriented towards caring for ''damaged'' people, meaning himself mostly. Sarah Donovan had come from a medical family. Her father had been a fine obstetrician, her brothers still practiced as medical specialists. Sarah herself had been a highly trained nurse. That was how they had met. Sarah had nursed Michael Donovan when he'd been invalided home. That was the start of a love affair that had survived many traumatic years.

Their mother had been the mainstay of the family. She had held them all in the palm of her hand, a born nurturer with tremendous reserves of good humour and patience. And hadn't she needed them! Carrie would never forget the dreadful day when she'd been called out of a lecture to be given the shattering news her mother had died very suddenly of a blood clot in the brain. The tragedy, coming as it did out of nowhere—her mother had been the healthiest and most energetic of women—instantly changed Carrie's life. She abandoned her ambitions to become a child psychologist to look after her distraught father and the twins, who couldn't cope with their grief. Fourteen was such a vulnerable age. Their father was no help. He turned more and more into himself. Carrie simply didn't have the heart to walk away.

Her selflessness had paid off. The boys, always brilliant students, were about to sit their first-year exams at med school in Brisbane. They had always wanted to be doctors from age six. Their mother's premature death had determined their career.

The familiar whooping wail that signalled the cyclone warning brought Carrie back. She turned up the volume, listening intently to the bulletin issued by the Bureau of Meteorology. No recent movements. What preoccupied her mind was when they should begin harvesting. She prayed her father was in good enough condition to make an early start home.

The bulletin over, Carrie switched off the radio and began preparing breakfast for Frank and Ben, bachelor brothers and loyal employees for almost twenty years. It was the least she could do. They'd been patrolling the plantation all night, making sure no would-be poachers had the opportunity to come in off the road and strip a few trees of the valuable fruit. It was becoming something of a problem, now the high-quality mangoes were fetching top prices on the domestic and overseas market.

By six o'clock the brothers were back, standing sheepishly at the back door. Frank, always the spokesman for the two, asked if her father was at home, knowing full well he wasn't. Ben scarcely said more than a half a dozen words before lapsing into silence.

"He's been staying in town of late, Frank."

"There's a decision to be made about harvesting, luvvy."

''I know.'' Carrie nodded. ''Dad will be home soon to decide. Anyway, come in. I've made breakfast for you both.''

''Smells good, too.'' Both men swept off their battered wide-brimmed hats and threw them onto a plant stand near the back door.

By mid-morning she'd made her own inspection of the plantation. The air under the canopy of trees was as thick and musky as the inside of a Buddhist temple. At least it was relatively cool. The sun had been making her dizzy. Bright and blinding, it appeared like an eerie, brazen catherine-wheel that actually seemed to be spinning slowly. Another effect of the strange cloud cover. The large pendulous fruit hung above her in their thousands—Kensington Pride. The dull green skin that would turn yellow with an attractive red blush when ripe. She was almost certain the crop was ready. Immature fruit wouldn't ripen naturally, that was the thing. It could be ripened under the influence of ethylene, but nobody wanted that. The result could be fruit of poor quality.

An hour later she sighted her father's four-wheel drive turn off the road. She rode swiftly towards the house, entering it a few minutes after him.

''Dad?'' she called, the nerves of her stomach tightening in anticipation of her father's mood and condition.

''Here, love.''

It occurred to her then, only two men's voices struck that chord deep inside her, her father's and Blake's. Both of them had dark timbred, very masculine voices with a resonant cutting edge.

Her father, a big man, was slumped at the kitchen table, head in hands, but tried to straighten as she entered.

''A cup of tea, Dad?'' she suggested, perturbed by the peculiar flush on his skin.

He shook his handsome head. "Don't bother, love. I had something at the pub. Sorry I didn't make it back last night. Had one too many."

"Dr. Richards warned you about your liver." Carrie took a chair opposite him.

"Doc's warned me about a lot of things. Most of which have come true." Michael Donovan fell silent, studying his daughter's worried face. "I'm not being fair to you, am I, love?" he asked eventually.

Carrie made a sympathetic sound. "You're not being fair to *yourself*, Dad."

His shapely mouth, slacked by drink, curled.

"That's my girl. Always loyal." Another brief silence. "I was finished, you know, the day your mother died," he said starkly.

Carrie leaned forward, clasping her father's hand. "I know your pain, Dad."

"No, love, you *don't*. You know *your* pain. It's different. Sarah was my wife. The best part of me. She pulled me through when I came home from Vietnam. She kept me more or less on course. She was the strong one."

Carrie's grip tightened. "Dad, you were decorated for *bravery*."

He shrugged it off with a movement of his powerful shoulders. "Pulling a mate out under fire isn't bravery, Carrie. It's doing what you have to do. You don't stop to think about it. You just *do* it."

"Well, Sandy Patterson is sure glad you did. So far as he's concerned, you're a hero. Why don't you believe it yourself?"

"Carrie, what did I actually do?" He groaned, running a hand through his thick hair. "Hell, love, I don't want to talk about it."

"You're so hard on yourself, Dad."

"You're like your mother," he said with a soft sigh. "You love me whatever. But I haven't responded too well under pressure. I was no good to you after your mother died. Not to you or the boys. *You* had to be the strong one. Nineteen years old. You gave up your studies when you're every bit as bright as the boys. Never a complaint. Never a minute of feeling sorry for yourself."

"Not that you *saw*, Dad. I threw a few cans in the shed."

"So you've got a temper. That's okay. You're like me." Michael Donovan suddenly started wringing his hands. "The thing is, Carrie, I've unravelled. I *know* it, but I can't seem to stop. Some days I get up intending to get things done. Intending to straighten myself out. Then the misery comes on me. *Why?* I ask myself. What the hell for?"

"How about me?" Carrie suggested. "You've got me, Dad. Sean and Steven love you."

"I know. They just don't know how to approach me, that's all. Not that I'm an approachable sort of chap." He smiled, showing a glimpse of his old charm. "I never drank like I'm drinking now. I've always gambled, but it never got out of hand. Since your mother left us I've made one wrong decision after the other. Sarah and I used to sit down and discuss things together. I always told her she was worth ten of me. She could run rings around me in business. Just like you. The thing is, I used to listen to her advice. Because you're my daughter, my *child*, I pig-headedly go ahead and back my own judgment. You know what happens a lot of the time. We lose out."

It was perfectly true, but still Carrie tried to offer comfort. "We'll have a good harvest, Dad. That will help."

"Ah! You don't know the half of it."

Carrie's stomach suddenly lurched. "Then you'd better tell me."

"I will. I will," he promised, rubbing his eyes. "We'll have a good talk later. Right now I need to lie down."

"We need to make a decision about the harvest. I've rung around this morning, and just about everyone agrees."

"Nervous nellies," Michael Donovan said shortly. "We haven't had a cyclone to really bother us in years."

"That could change."

He pushed his chair back in extreme irritation. "What do you want, then? For me to go down on my knees praying?"

"Give the okay to start picking."

"Why don't we just flip a coin," he suggested. "That would make sense."

"There could be a crisis, Dad." Carrie kept her tone quiet.

He looked down at her, his face giving out contradictory signals, a desire to take positive action and the inability to do so.

"All right, love," he said finally. "You're as good a judge as any, but the crop isn't really *fully* mature."

"It's right to harvest, Dad," she offered her considered opinion. "There's a problem, though, and there won't be enough packers to go round."

"Call out the Army," Michael Donovan said flippantly, his handsome face slack with drink and fatigue. "Failing that, go see your boyfriend."

"You mean Tim?" Carrie's eyebrows shot up in surprise.

Michael Donovan gave a short bark, "You're smarter than that. I mean Blake Courtland. Who else? Tim's a simple country bumpkin beside Blake."

"Blake's hardly my boyfriend," Carrie said in some amazement.

"Then what the hell is he doing over here?" Michael Donovan shook his head in disgust. "He fancies you, all right. And why wouldn't he? You're as bright as a button, you have your mother's caring nature and you're as beautiful as a rose. Sometimes I think you don't believe in yourself any more than I do."

Carrie opened her mouth to protest, then shut it. Her father had never said such things before. "Blake was in love with Amanda, Dad," she said finally, as though that settled it. "He was about to marry her. Most people think he still hasn't gotten over his grief."

"What grief he's had he can handle." Michael Donovan shrugged philosophically. "You've only got to look at Blake to know he's a man of strong passions. Forget that smooth cover. It's only insulation. Besides, I don't know that he was that much in love with that poor girl. They'd been thrown together for years, families and so forth. Sir Talbot and Lady Courtland smiled benevolently upon her."

"She was lovely, Dad. I remember her."

"And so she was," Michael Donovan agreed. "Which is more than can be said for that snotty-nosed sister of hers. She always looks so cold she must have an in-built refrigerator. No, to my way of thinking there was no great passion on Blake's side. I'm not saying he didn't care about her. I'm sure he did, but she wasn't destined to be the love of his life, like your mother was mine. I never looked at another woman from the day I met Sarah." He walked to the door, looking back at Carrie. "Why don't you dress yourself up a bit? You'd be beautiful if you only took a little trouble. And why that blessed pigtail? You have glorious hair. Take it from your old dad. Blake Courtland is well aware of you. Even when you're talking about something as mundane as the weather, the air crackles around you. Do you think I'm so stupid I haven't noticed?"

"You've never actually said anything."

"No, but there could be a few changes around here."

Carrie looked at her father carefully, aware he was at the end of his tether. "I'll only go to Blake in an emergency. No matter what you say, I think he has a problem seeing me as anyone else but young Carrie Donovan."

"Carolyn. He always calls you Carolyn," her father corrected her. "Sounds good, as a matter of fact."

"Is there anything I can get you, Dad?"

"Maybe a couple of pain-killers. Strictly speaking, I suppose I should have my stomach pumped."

Her father was lying down when she brought the medication to him. He took the two white tablets, holding them in his palm. "I'm sorry, Carrie. I really am. You're wasting your life sticking by me. Lord knows I'm drinking myself to death. Something that genuinely surprises me. I used to dislike whisky once, but the taste comes if you work at it." He swallowed the tablets and handed the glass back. "The boys have gone off. Pagets, both of them. I should be grateful. They'll make a success of their lives. Probably marry another set of identical twins. They have a lot to thank *you* for. Don't let them ever forget it."

"Dad, they sing my praises," Carrie pointed out with perfect truth.

"So they should. I could drop dead, for all they care. None of this is fair to *you*. You deserve your life back, Carrie."

"I can finish off my course, Dad. I'm only twenty-three."

"I'm the stumbling block," he murmured. "You worry too much about what's going to happen to me."

She bent to kiss his forehead. "Of course I do. I love you."

"I think that's what keeps me alive. I love you, too, Carrie, except I'm no good to you at all."

Carrie was startled at the depth of feeling in her father's voice. "Dad," she said fervently. "Would you let someone help you? You don't have to go it alone."

He shook his head wryly. "Whisky is the best medicine. It dulls the tearing pain. Nothing will bring your mother back. What happened to her happened to me. That's the thing most people can't seem to understand. I'm blessed or cursed with a faithful heart. In that way you're like me, Carrie. When you love you'll love forever."

"Try to get some sleep, Dad," Carrie said gently. "I'll get things underway."

Michael Donovan closed his eyes, beginning to sing a few lines from the old nursery rhyme.

"And all the king's horses and all the king's men couldn't put Donovan back together again."

Carrie, listening at the doorway, thought her heart might break.

CHAPTER TWO

BY THE time Blake returned, Carrie had finished afternoon tea. She hadn't realized how hungry she was until it arrived. The little lemon cream slices had simply melted in her mouth.

"Sorry about that," Blake apologised, his eyes making an approving sweep of the silver tray. "We've had an update on Anita. She's on the move. Southward at around fifteen kilometres per hour. We just have to keep our fingers crossed she doesn't make any westerly swings toward the coast."

It seemed to Carrie such an imposition to bother him. He had *huge* responsibilities. A station to look after. Abruptly she stood up. "Look, I'm sorry about this. I shouldn't have come here. You have enough to worry about without us." There was strain in her voice. Something deeper.

"Let's put that aside for a moment, shall we?" he asked her firmly. "You suffer from the sin of pride, Carolyn Donovan."

"I know."

"And beyond that, something to do with me."

She shrugged. "Maybe. It's too complicated. I can't explain."

"We can't go into it now. But sometime we're going to have to," he told her bluntly. "As far as the station's concerned, we're already on alert. Fully prepared. I've made enquiries about the plantations, as well. They'll begin an immediate harvest. The mayor's gone off to

112

marshal some manpower. The local pickers won't be able to manage.''

''No, of course not.'' For once she let her eyes linger on his, saturating herself in their blueness. ''We'd be terribly grateful for any help we can get.''

He gave a faintly ironic smile. ''Couldn't you look at me like that all the time?''

There it was again the blue leap of flame. ''Blake, you're making me nervous.''

''Nobody makes *you* nervous, Carolyn.''

''*You* do. You know you do. It happens all the time.''

''So what are we talking about now? Silent communication?''

She looked away, unable to prevent the sudden rush of delicate colour to her skin. ''It *can* happen.''

''Oh, I know that *now*,'' he replied dryly. ''But let's talk about something a lot easier. Mick's at home today?''

Instantly she was on the defensive. ''Yes. He's not terribly well, though.''

Blake made some sort of gesture with his hand. Pity? Disgust? Enough to make her throat tighten, but all he said was, ''I'm sorry to hear that, Carolyn. These past years have been hard for him. Hard for you, too. I take it you've discussed it, though. He's prepared to go to harvest?''

''We realise the consequences if we don't.''

''Knowing Mick, it's a wonder he didn't say the cyclone could bugger off.''

''Actually, he did.''

''You love your father, don't you?''

''Of course I do.'' The light in her eyes changed. Became tender. ''He's not a happy man, but he's still got some magic in him.''

''That he has, and he's passed it on.'' Abruptly Blake moved towards the huge mahogany partner's desk. ''If

Mick's given the okay, it would be best to start harvesting this afternoon.'' He picked up the phone. "I need to make a call. It occurred to me last night you'd need help. I started to organise something then."

"Do you overlook *anything*?" Carrie asked.

One eyebrow shot up. "I sometimes can't guess what *you* might do."

"I'm not surprised." Her smile was rueful. "You have an unsettling effect on me."

"Don't think I'm not aware of it." He began to dial a number, then spoke into the phone, keeping his voice low.

In a few moments it was arranged, and a heavy burden was lifted from Carrie's shoulders. Blake had marshalled a small army, including a fair percentage of their usual pickers, who would show the new recruits what to do.

As he put down the phone Carrie moved towards him, her mind filled with all the things he had done for them. "Dad and I can't thank you enough, Blake." Words weren't adequate, so gracefully she offered him her hand.

He looked at it for a moment before taking it in his own. "What if I need more?"

For a long moment she couldn't move. This was far beyond anything he had ever said before. Not just the words, but the way he said them, so deep and quiet yet with so much fire. Had she heard him at all? Or was his voice inside her head again? One of those silent moments of communication that both thrilled and troubled her.

Blake continued to look at her with such infinite intensity it set her whole being alight. Never in her life had she felt such a surge of shock and excitement. It beat in her veins like fiery wings. It wasn't something commonplace he was asking. A neighbourly gesture. It was significant. A commitment.

Even as she began to believe there really were miracles, uncertainty invaded her. The cold light of reason continued to haunt her. Did it take only a few disturbing words from him to cast her into a ferment? Was Blake Courtland, one of the most powerful and influential men in the state, hitherto not just out of reach but unattainable, so interested in her he had reached the point where he was going to declare it? What if he had something less binding in mind? A casual affair would shatter her. Misinterpretation would cover her in such embarrassment their lifelong friendship could be ended.

Carrie averted her head, afraid if she looked at him for only a second longer her eyes would betray her. "Blake, I—don't quite—"

He turned her face to him, his hand on her cheek setting up such a blood rush she felt dizzy. His blue eyes blazed. Burned. "You can't run away forever, Carolyn. You're a woman now."

And an innocent, she felt like pleading. An innocent with very little experience. It would be strange to him, the consummate man of the world. "I didn't think you saw me in that way," she said in a low voice. It wasn't precisely true, but it was a defence of some kind.

"Be truthful, Carolyn. Haven't there been moments?" He kept his burning eyes trained on her, not letting her escape.

And such moments! she thought. Wild, improbable, splendid, but always that sense of heightened unreality. Suppressing her importunate feelings about Blake Courtland had become second nature. Only for tragedy he would have been married by now. His beautiful Amanda would have taken him away from her forever. Love wasn't only a delight. It was a torment.

"There *is* communication between us, Blake," she admitted unsteadily. "I can't deny it. We've always got on well together." That, to trivialise the magic! But it was a desperate attempt to put the initiative back on him.

His eyes rested on the throbbing pulse in her throat. He dropped his hand, and the intensity of his manner eased. "So we have," he agreed in his usual smooth, confident tone. "Let's see, how long have I known you?"

Carrie released her breath, feeling relief and a measure of composure. "I have a clear recollection of you when I was about five." The vision still occupied her mind's eye. "You were riding a wonderful palomino. *Such* a horse! You leaned down sideways in the saddle to say a few words to the little Donovan girl. I thought you quite marvellous. A young god. Not like us ordinary folk at all." Her tender mouth turned ironic. "Not a lot's changed."

He made a faintly scoffing sound. "I can't possibly agree with that. A great deal has changed. Don't ever underestimate your own worth, Carolyn. You weren't ordinary then and you're not now. Be honest about things."

"I try to be." She gave a little sigh, almost sad. "But we still lead very different lives, Blake. You're a man who has everything. For us life has become one long, hard grind."

His handsome face tightened. "Do you think I don't know that? I know the whole situation. You're immensely loyal to your father, Carolyn, and I applaud it. You've practically sacrificed your life, your ambitions for your brothers, but you can't allow all that caring to destroy your chance at happiness. You have to start to live for yourself."

What he was saying she had thought many times herself, yet it stung her. "So what is it you think I should do?" She turned on him, her eyes iridescent emeralds.

"Why so hostile?" he countered. "Do you think I'm intruding too deeply into your affairs?"

A kind of grief rose in her throat. "You've helped us so much. I never wanted—" She broke off abruptly, feeling a biting sense of obligation.

"Don't." It was said almost tenderly.

"But it's true, Blake." She threw up her head. "I know Dad has approached you for loans. I know you've given them to him. I know we haven't paid them back."

"Surely you're not going to hate me for it?"

"No, no. How could you think that?"

"It's not unusual for someone to resent the person they have to turn to for help."

"It's not like that at all, Blake. But I have to admit it's a source of constant sorrow."

"Which is why you're becoming increasingly guarded with me? Is that it? It's quite obvious you don't want me to get too close."

It was unnerving how he had hit on the truth. "I'm not looking to play with fire, Blake," she explained.

"When fire is your nature?" His eyes rested on her glowing, dark red hair, the sparkly green eyes. "Even your coloring is full of radiance."

"I'm properly cautious." She cast him a grave look. "Perhaps you've overlooked that?"

"I don't think so." His voice was very dry. "On the contrary, I've paid a bit too much attention to it. I think the time's come—" He stopped abruptly as someone came very quietly to stand at the door. "Ah, Diane, there you are!" Suavely he slipped into his social guise.

"I'm leaving now, Blake." Diane was frowning, her delicate nostrils quivering as though scenting the intensity in the air.

"I am, too." Carrie didn't know how, but she managed to sound fairly normal.

"Good. I'll walk with you to your car." Diane entered the room briskly, then stood on tiptoe to kiss Blake's cheek. "Until Saturday," she murmured with soft urgency.

"Providing Cyclone Anita doesn't come in." The matter-of-factness of his tone caused the suggestion of intimacy to fall flat.

Blake transferred his blue gaze to Carrie. "Tell Mick I'll be over to see him when I get the chance. It's going to be a hectic time for you even with all the help."

"Thanks again, Blake," Carrie said with quiet gratitude, watching a staff member approach. Blake had an urgent phone call. He excused himself, and the two young women walked down the steps together.

"Surely you're not asking for Blake's help *again*, are you?" Diane's voice fairly cracked with scorn.

"Why should that put *you* out?" Carrie asked mildly.

"Can't you handle things yourself? Blake has far too many responsibilities. I would have thought you would appreciate that."

"This is an emergency, Diane. Just as I said."

Diane shot her a dark look. "I think it's just another excuse for you to come around."

"You think so?"

"Oh, don't act the innocent. I know so."

"But it's not actually your business, is it?"

"Of course it is," Diane maintained flatly, then added the strangest thing. "It's not that long since Mandy died."

Carrie found the remark upsetting. "I'm afraid I don't follow." She stood stock-still, staring into Diane's face.

"I don't think you're that obtuse. I see the way you look at Blake."

Inwardly Carrie winced. "I admire him. I'm sure that's nothing to hide."

"They'd have been married," Diane said, ignoring her comment. "Probably had a child. A handsome little boy who looked just like Blake." A shadow rushed over her face.

"I didn't know Amanda all that well," Carrie said gently. "She was older, but whenever I did meet her I thought her quite lovely."

"So how could he forget a woman like that?" Diane asked with great bitterness.

Carrie looked at the young woman with pity. "I'm sure he hasn't." Finally, mercifully, they were at the Jeep.

"So don't *you* forget it, either." Diane was all jagged edges. "I recognise an opportunist when I see one."

"But you're quite wrong," Carrie said with dignity. "What would you call yourself, I wonder? Do you have to do your hair in exactly Amanda's style? I would have thought it would be hurtful for all of you."

Diane stiffened in outrage. "It's a tribute! A reminder that Amanda will never be forgotten."

"Forgive me if I have a more enquiring mind."

"Since you mention it, Blake *likes* it," Diane answered resolutely.

"I can't believe that."

"You just don't *want* to believe it." Diane's cool face blazed. "I know I can never match Amanda or take her place in his heart, but she was my sister. We're a lot alike. Blake has come to realise that."

Confirmation at last! Carrie had often thought Diane Anthony was in love with Blake. Even when her sister had been alive.

"You'll have to excuse me, Diane," she said kindly, feeling a little afraid for the young woman. "I must get back to the plantation."

"Surely farm would be a better description?" Diane let out a scornful laugh. "The real plantations are considerably bigger than yours."

"Trust me, it's a plantation."

"Well, take care of yourself." Diane reverted to a mock friendly tone. "Lovely to chat. It's not really fair your brothers having all the advantages. You work so hard and you're so *thin*. The problems with your father wouldn't help. I do *feel* for you. Someone was only saying the other night your father had gone downhill terribly since your mother died."

Carrie ignored the callous taunt. "*You* must know what it's like living without someone you love." She started the engine then looked down. "You're right when you say you can never match Amanda."

Even then Carrie didn't have the last word. Diane stood back from the Jeep with a look of jaunty confidence. "It seems to me I have a far better chance than *you*, Carrie dear. You're the battling farmhand. Not me."

The following morning Michael Donovan still wasn't well enough to oversee the harvesting on his plantation. He seemed to be in pain, snapping at Carrie in the somewhat irrational way he had. It was obviously best she kept out of his way. The bulk of Blake's army, bussed in from another town, had arrived in force, but even then the workload was great. A low ceiling of thick clouds, advance runners of the cyclone, hung right over the entire district, and the rain was coming down. By mid-morning one of the helpers unfamiliar with the hydraulically operated platforms used to harvest had an accident, and a doctor had to be called to give him treatment.

The job went on. Pickers moved steadily from tree to tree, harvesting by hand or using long picking sticks with a catching bag. As Carrie had anticipated with the newcomers, there were burns from the caustic sap. They were using the trampolines filled with water to wash the sap from the stems, but there simply weren't enough to go around. At least they didn't have to worry about a hot sun damaging the fruit. For the time being, the wet, cooler conditions were allowing the pickers to work at a faster rate. All of them felt that sense of urgency. Cyclone Anita had changed direction during the night, moving slowly but inexorably towards the coast.

From dawn to dusk they barely stopped. At dusk, when they could no longer remain in the fields, work was stopped until first light the next morning. Carrie had prepared a herbed pork and spinach terrine for Frank and Ben, which they'd happily made off with, but she thought pasta and a salad would do for her and her father. Not that Michael Donovan had his hearty appetite anymore. These days a bottle of whisky was the perfect food.

Carrie showered and washed her hair in the en suite adjoining the main bedroom. *Her* bedroom now. It had been her parents', but her father couldn't bear to sleep there anymore. He had taken over the spare room and the adjoining sewing room, knocking a wall out to enlarge the space.

She changed into fresh clothes, a ribbed cotton knit tank top and cotton jeans. In the humid heat her hair sprang into a million curls and deep waves. Pre-Raphaelite, her mother had called it. Carrie thought it just plain wild. She went to tie it back then decided to leave it. It still wasn't dry.

Some time later, when she was washing lettuce at the kitchen sink, she heard a car drive in from the road. Hurriedly she wiped her hands on a tea towel and went to the door.

Blake.

Like always, her heart rocked. "Dad, Blake's here," she called, trying to control the excitement that nevertheless vibrated in her voice.

The response was predictably dry. "Sit him down, m'darlin'. I'll be out in a few moments."

There was a large, oval mirror above the hallstand.
Carrie couldn't resist a quick glance into it, startled by
the brilliance of her eyes against the cream of her skin.
Never in her life had her mother allowed her to go out
in the sun without a hat. It had paid off. She didn't even
have a freckle. Her hair looked almost wired, every
strand quivering and dancing, but it couldn't be helped.

Blake was already at the front door. A dynamic
presence. He was wearing a raincoat, which he took off
immediately, but his hair and skin were slick with rain.

"Hang on a moment and I'll get you a towel." Did
she have to make it sound a matter of life and death?

"Don't bother. I'm okay," he told her carelessly and
drew a handkerchief from his pocket and rubbed it over
his face and head. "It's going to get worse. A lot worse,
I'm afraid."

"It seems so." Carrie gazed at the heavy sheets of water
that curtained the garden in silver. "Come in out of the
downpour, Blake," she urged, beginning to shut the
door. "Thanks to you, we did marvellously well today.
Everyone worked so hard. Dad and I are immensely
grateful." Her nervous fingers touched his arm lightly.
"He'll be here in a moment."

"You said that like we need a chaperon." His tone
was intimate, warm, amused.

"I didn't mean *that*," she protested, feeling her cheeks
flush.

"Of course you didn't," he said, relenting. "I've never
known you to be deliberately provocative. I'm only
teasing."

"You're terribly good at it." She glanced up quickly,
only to find him studying her with an undeniably ad-
miring expression. "What is it?"

"All that pre-Raphaelite hair." He reached out, let a
long lock slide through his fingers, waited for it to spring

back. A casual enough gesture, yet it kindled in Carrie a warm rush of pleasure.

"It's a bit wild," she said. "I've just washed it. It takes a day or two to settle down." *Stop babbling,* she thought, but too many sensations were crowding her.

"A better crowning glory is hard to imagine. A man would find it hard to keep his hands off it." He looked down at her from his superior height, such quiet power in his superbly fit body. Her legs turned to wax. "Sweet Carolyn," he murmured, lingering over her name.

"You're in a very good mood," she said, a little shakily.

"It could have something to do with you."

She didn't utter a word but looked away from him carefully as though the sight of him dazzled her. "Would you like to come through to the kitchen? I'm preparing tea."

"Lead the way, Miss Donovan," he invited. "I'll check out your culinary skills while we talk."

"I'm quite a good cook," she said over her shoulder. "But not up to the standard of your Kai."

"Kai does it for a living," Blake said in a casual voice. "He had his own restaurant before he came to me. I couldn't do without him for all the entertaining."

Inside the large kitchen he was so tall, so vital, he made the room seem claustrophobic.

"Sit down, Blake," Carrie said, trying not to sound as off balance as she felt. "Could I offer you something?"

"A cold beer if you have it." He pulled out a chair, so handsome in the bright light he took her breath away. "I've been solidly on the go for the past fourteen hours."

"What about something to eat with it?" she suggested quickly, knowing the extent of his responsibilities.

"Carolyn, I thought you'd never ask." His blue eyes were filled with a kind of devilment.

"You mean you'd like to stay to tea?"

"I think it would be a great idea." His mouth quirked. "But only if you want me."

Didn't he know it was bliss to have him there? Bliss mixed up with those nagging prohibitions. "You're very welcome," she said with unconscious sweetness. "I thought you might have been expected home." She made a little spiralling movement of her hand, which he followed with his eyes.

"How incredibly graceful you are. The way you stand, the way you move. Even the way you balance on one foot. I always expect you to break into an arabesque."

"You'd like to see one?" She was only joking, yet thinking of all those years she had studied ballet at her mother's insistence.

"I'd do *anything* to see one." Laughter brackets accentuated his beautifully cut mouth.

"Are you serious?" she asked in some surprise.

"Of course. Why would you doubt me?"

"Well, not everyone asks. As a matter of fact, not a lot of people know I studied ballet." With one hand on the kitchen counter for support, Carrie went immediately into a graceful arabesque, her right leg supporting her body, her left leg extended behind her to a considerable height.

Blake gave her a little round of applause. "I haven't seen better on stage. Now I remember a pigtailed kid in a leotard."

"Eight years," she said nostalgically, resuming her normal stance. "Mum insisted if I was going to be tall I had to have good posture."

The blue eyes moved over her like a lick of flame. "Well, the ballet paid off, without a doubt."

The atmosphere was becoming so highly charged it was almost unbreathable. "How am I going to handle all these compliments?" Carrie asked.

"Accept them as gracefully as you do everything else. You might try saying something nice to me for a change."

"Nothing could be easier." She spoke earnestly. "You're the best neighbour anyone could possibly wish for. The most generous. The most supportive. I truly mean it, though I know I don't show it all the time."

He made a little impatient sound. "That's all very commendable, Carolyn, but would you care to add something a little more *personal*?"

She looked up, startled. "I can't imagine life without you." It came out spontaneously, before her defence system had time to work. *My God!* she thought. *What have I said?*

"That's very impressive for an opener," Blake congratulated her smoothly. "The thing is, do you mean it?"

The tension was mounting so swiftly Carrie sought to calm herself. She turned away to the cupboard, setting out extra dishes with much too much clatter.

"Well?" he prompted, sounding as though he was about to stop her.

Carrie swallowed convulsively. "I do. In lots of ways."

"Lord!" Blake groaned. "Do I have to drag it out of you? Name a few."

There was so much challenge in his voice her hand shook. "What are you trying to do to me, Blake?"

"I told you," he returned a little tersely. "Shake you up. Make you confront things as they are."

"I think I do." Her graceful body was very still. "I have a very clear picture of you. You're someone from another world. Someone truly exceptional. You're the owner of a very grand station. Your entire clan is proud of you, happy to see you hold the reins of power. You're practically worshipped in the district. And for good reason, I must add. You're Blake Courtland. You have it all."

"You think so?" The vibrant voice fairly rasped.

"I know so." Without realising it, she clasped a hand to her heart. "You've known tragedy. You've had your dreams shattered. I haven't forgotten that. Never. But you've risen above it all. I feel I'm still little Carrie Donovan, the child, the teenager you were always so nice to. An ordinary, hardworking girl from one of the plantations. Not that you've ever called me Carrie. Not once."

"Carolyn is a beautiful name," he said. "You're a beautiful young woman. You're also highly intelligent. I did take note of all the high grades. Your mother especially was very proud of you."

"I miss her terribly."

"I know," he said gently. "I know, too, she wouldn't want you to waste your life."

"You think I'm doing that?" She was stung afresh.

"You're made for marriage, Carolyn," he said in a taut, challenging voice. "To be a wife and mother. Have a home of your own. You need someone to love you. Someone to truly appreciate all you have to offer."

Her heart was beating so rapidly she felt giddy. "One of these days I might meet my Prince Charming. Or he'll find me."

"He'll have to, if you won't open your eyes. Look at me, Carolyn."

"I think I have to psyche myself up for it," she admitted in a rueful voice.

"What are you afraid of?"

She turned her face to him. His eyes were exactly the colour of sapphires. Drawing out her soul. "Taking on too much for me to handle." *Giving myself up to you. Losing myself completely. Perhaps forever.* She had always associated him with prestige and power. The Diane Anthonys of this world. Diane was still there. Waiting, as she had always been, in the wings.

"Where's your sense of daring?" he scoffed. "I would have thought you very courageous."

"Maybe I have the sense to shy off when the risks are too great."

"What risks? What are you talking about now?"

"You're disturbing me thoroughly, Blake."

"You'll survive it." He gave her a mocking smile.

"I never realised what a tease you are."

"Come on, Carolyn. I'm talking sense."

"I don't want to interrupt anything," Michael Donovan said from the kitchen door, his sardonic glance going from one to the other.

"We've got a visitor, Dad." Carrie willed her heart to slow.

"And a very welcome one, too. Blake, good to see you."

Blake stood up and the two men shook hands.

"Carolyn's kindly asked me to tea, Mick. I hope that's okay with you."

"It's an honour." Michael Donovan waved the younger man into his chair. "I need to thank you personally for arranging so much help for us."

"No problem, Mick. As long as it's been effective."

"And so it has. Everyone's worked very hard, including yours truly. Now, what are we having, Carrie?" Light-heartedly, Michael Donovan put an arm around his daughter's narrow waist, not altogether surprised to find she was trembling.

"Pasta, Dad, with a salad." She leaned against him briefly.

"Then I'd best go and find us a nice chardonnay. It's good to have company. It's much too quiet for Carrie these days," he added pointedly.

They ate in the dining room, where Carrie had quickly whipped up an attractive informal setting, placing yellow roses centre table. The yellow picked up the yellow stripe in the linen table napkins and the yellow pears in the fruit decoration around the rim of the plates.

For once her father ate with appetite, clearly enjoying Blake's company and appreciative of a good audience for his fund of funny stores. Carrie watched them both with a mixture of feelings, pleasure, pain and that queer, all-pervading sense of unreality. Her father had believed for some time Blake was interested in her. It now appeared he was right. But in what way? Was it true she actually feared their changing relationship? Feared to achieve an impossible dream?

The meal went off well despite the drumming of the rain on the corrugated iron roof and the swirl of undercurrents that never left them. They had coffee in the living room, and an hour later Blake rose to his feet, saying he would call in some time the following day. Michael Donovan saw him out.

It was still raining at dawn, but everyone to a man was assembled to continue the harvest, which was never destined to be completed. At noon Michael Donovan came back to the fields from the house, face and voice tense. "Dangerous winds expected," he told Carrie briefly before moving on to inform the workers.

Cyclone Anita had made a sharp turn during the day, picking up on the severity scale. It was highly probable they would lose around a tenth of the crop, but the high winds even then were making it dangerous and uncomfortable work. By mid-afternoon Blake arrived. He caught up with Carrie where she was working, almost exhausted and drenched to the skin. His expression turned grim. He put a hard, detaining hand to her arm, preventing her from continuing.

"You'll have to call this off, Carolyn. Conditions are bad. A lot of branches and debris are getting airborne. They could turn into missiles. Where the devil's Mick?"

He turned his head sharply, looking around. The rain glistened off his raven hair and coppered skin. There was a vertical line between his black brows, giving him a most daunting aspect.

"Dad had to go back to the house," Carrie cried over the tempest. "I don't know what's wrong with him. He'll *never* tell me."

"This has to stop," Blake repeated with some force. "You look like you're on the point of collapse. I'll tell the men to get off home. They'll be glad to."

"*I'll* tell the men." Doggedly she went to turn, but found herself staggering instead.

"Do I need to say any more? Rest here a moment, *please*." He settled her against the wood platform then swung away, the very picture of male toughness and authority.

In no time the order to cease work spread through the plantation. The workers started to come in, downing their tools in the bins, then racing to their cars and vans. It was obvious they were only too grateful to call it a day. Most of them had properties to secure.

Frank and Ben were the last to leave, making it their business to look after the equipment and lock the sheds. The wind had picked up unbelievably. For all her jumbled feelings, Carrie had to acknowledge Blake had done the right thing. She should have made the decision herself, only she was so physically exhausted she didn't seem to be functioning properly.

"Let's get into the house." Blake got his arm around her, half turning her to him so he could shelter her from the whirling clouds of leaves, dirt and twigs. It was obvious he was angry and disturbed. She could feel it in the heat that emanated from him.

They were halfway between the plantation of trees and the homestead when a sheet of corrugated iron was suddenly lifted without warning from one of the packing

sheds and came hurtling at them like a lethal weapon
thrown by a giant.

Blake saw it first, feeling a jolt of horror. He had an
instant decision to make—forward or back towards the
trees. The wind appeared to be coming from all direc-
tions. He hoped long experience allowed him to gauge
correctly the main force. With a galvanic thrust, he pro-
pelled them towards the garden at a run, half lifting,
half dragging a near-exhausted Carrie out of the judged
path of flight.

Carrie could feel the fear and panic rise in her throat.
Incidents like this could and did kill people, a neighbour
not that many years before. She went down hard as Blake
flung them to the ground, her head and body pressed
into the thick, wet grass. She was almost choking on
blades of it. Blake's hard, muscled body lay across her,
forming a human shield. The air whistled and screamed
as the silver sheet sailed some distance clear of them,
airborne but about to drop to earth.

It wasn't until they heard it crash into the side of the
large carport used for additional parking that Blake lifted
his head.

"What the hell goes on around here?" he demanded
violently of no one. "Mick was to get that roofing *fixed*."
Swiftly he turned Carrie over, staring into her face. She
had her eyes closed, and her translucent skin had never
seemed whiter. He brushed a long strand of wet dark
red hair from her brow. "You're not hurt, are you?" he
asked urgently. "There was no time to be gentle."

"Only breathless." Gingerly Carrie tried to move. The
forced descent had almost knocked the air from her
lungs. *What now?* she thought, meeting Blake's blazing
gaze. What had her father done with the money Blake
had loaned him? Humiliation was like the fierce jab of
a needle.

"I can't afford to let you lie there." Blake rose quickly, assisting her to her feet. "I'll take you to the house, then I'll have to fix that sheet of iron. It could take off again."

"Don't say anything, Blake, *please*," she begged.

He hesitated, obviously not wanting to upset her. "Carolyn, Mick has to do something about himself."

"I know, I know, but please don't start."

"Really, have I ever done that?" His voice was harsh. "You're *angry*."

"Why is that such a surprise?" he demanded. "Maybe Mick doesn't care about himself, but he *has* to care about you. You've nearly reached the end of your tether."

"I'm tired and wet. That's all. Don't worry about me. I'll make it to the house. If you could secure that sheet, I'd be grateful. You could put it in the garage. It's not locked."

"It's *crucial* these things are attended to," Blake muttered as he stalked away.,

Inside the house, Carrie stripped off her wet clothes and changed before she looked in on her father. He was resting on his bed, his eyes closed.

"Dad?" she called in a soft but urgent voice.

"What is it? What's up?" His eyes flew open, and he struggled to sit up.

"Nothing. Don't worry. We've had to call off work. Conditions are too bad. What's wrong with you, Dad? You must tell me."

"I'm ill," he said and fell back.

Carrie approached the bed, pale from shock and concern. She leaned over, searching her father's face. "Where?"

"All over." Michael Donovan gave a mirthless laugh. "I could have *anything*, I suppose. No one could exactly say I've been looking after myself."

"Are you in pain?" Carrie asked, reaching down to feel his forehead. His skin was cool, faintly clammy. Not hot.

"I was. Not now. It could be these damned gallstones. Remember I was supposed to have the op?"

"There were lots of things you were supposed to have, Dad, but you never got around to it. The thing is, a bad situation might be forced on us. I think we should get you to hospital. It would be terrible if you had an attack during the cyclone. The pain is supposed to be horrendous."

"I know all about pain, my darlin'." Her father gave a grim smile.

"I know you do, but you can't afford to be foolish. Besides, you're worrying me to death."

"Then may God forgive me." Michael Donovan sighed. "You've been a daughter and son to me, Carrie. You've worked so hard. Look at you! A bag of bones. And your hair's sopping wet."

"It's raining outside, Dad," Carrie said patiently. "Blake's here."

Michael Donovan froze in shock. "What, in the house?"

"He's securing something outside."

"Surely Frank or Ben did that?"

"Perhaps we haven't been careful enough. He'll be here in a moment."

"I remember I should have had a few things fixed." Michael Donovan's gaze turned rueful then defensive. "Tell him I'm ill. Tell him that."

"I've already told him. Knowing Blake, you don't think he's just going to accept that and walk away?"

"This is *my* home. And that's a fact." A vein pulsed in his forehead. "What's happening to me, girl?"

"It's as plain as it could be we have to find out. You're taking awful risks with your life. I'm afraid for you,

Dad,'' Carrie said softly, stopping as she heard Blake's voice.

"Now that's the man himself!" her father said. "Go to him, love. Explain."

"Blake will think the same as I do, Dad. This pain has to be checked out. And today. Conditions are worsening all the time."

"I'll be all right, love." For once Michael Donovan sounded unsure of it.

"I'll be back in a moment," Carrie promised. "Don't be surprised if Blake comes with me."

Blake was standing in the hallway. He had left his raincoat on the veranda and was making a few desultory efforts to dry his head. "What's wrong with Mick?" His voice was still terse.

"That's what I'm going to find out. He said he was in pain but it's gone away now. I don't believe him. It could be his gall bladder. He was supposed to have an operation two years ago."

"If that's the case we'd better get him to hospital. And right now. Before it gets impossible to drive."

"Could you speak to him? He seems to take things from you."

"At least someone does." Blake followed her as she led the way down the corridor to her father's room. He took one look at Michael Donovan's sick, ravaged face and said flatly, "Mick, you can't let this go on. Carolyn is desperately worried about you. So am I."

"So what do you suggest?" Michael Donovan abruptly became solemn.

"A quick trip to the hospital. Carolyn can get a few things together, then we'll leave. This could be your life we're talking about here."

"Are you taking me then?" Michael Donovan asked, sounding oddly relieved.

"I can take Dad, Blake," Carrie offered with some effort. She was sore and shaky from their experience.

Blake turned from the bed, looking as though he had come to the end of his patience. "Carolyn, I wouldn't hear of it. It might even be better if you stayed safely in the house."

"I'm not going to do that!" He green eyes flared. "You heard me, Blake," she added when it looked like he was going to come down even harder. "I'll put some things together in an overnight bag. It will take me five minutes."

It was a harrowing journey into town, and a worse one coming back with darkness set in and visibility poor. Michael Donovan had been admitted for observation while his doctor all but rubbed his hands together in satisfaction. This time, such a recalcitrant patient was not going to get away.

Blake brought the station wagon to a halt at the bottom of the steps. Even then the wind-driven rain lashed at them as they raced onto the veranda. It was impossible to keep dry.

The electricity was still on. Carrie flicked a switch while Blake pushed the door hard against the howling wind. Water had entered the house, running in a rivulet up the polished floor and dampening the Indian rug.

"Carolyn, I can't leave you here," he said with some urgency.

She was making her way up the hall towards the living room, switching on lights as she went. She turned, looking all of a sudden very fragile. "You've done everything anyone could possibly expect, Blake. You must go home now. I can't keep you from your responsibilities. I'm worried it will be a terrible drive for you."

"I'd better ring the house. That's if I can get a call through." He moved purposefully towards the phone, looking surprised to get a dial tone.

"I'll check the back of the house." Carrie moved off so he could make his call in peace.

A few minutes later Blake joined her as she went about securing the storm shutters.

"Here, let me do that. You're starting to look like the wind will blow you over." He sounded taut, uncharacteristically edgy. "It looks like you'll have company tonight."

Her heart lurched. "You mean you're staying?"

His eyes raked her, blue as forked lightning. "No cause for alarm, surely? It so happens a big tree has come down at Bangara Crossing. It's lying right across the road. Just missed the power lines, I'm told. I don't fancy a walk from there."

"Of course not." She managed to sound understanding, when all the time she felt she was unravelling. "In any case it's too dangerous on the road. I'm so sorry, Blake. We're getting to lean on you too hard."

"Am I complaining?" he asked a touch shortly.

"You've a right to."

His smile tensed. "Don't start getting too grateful to me. Not now."

"But I *am* grateful to you," she said emotionally, and paused to regain control. "You saved my life."

"Doesn't that mean our souls are locked together forever?"

"Some people believe that."

"You don't?"

Tension hung around them like a heavy cloak. Even with the wildness outside, the atmosphere inside the house was heat-charged, explosive. If he touched her, Carrie thought. *If he touched her.* She would go up in flames. Her whole body was quivering. They were quite alone. Both of them shaken by the events of the day. Anything could happen.

The silence lengthened, deepened as he looked at her. The sound and fury of the rain drumming relentlessly against all sides of the house paled to insignificance beside his powerful magnetism. She fancied she swayed towards him. Had she? A moment later the house was thrown into utter darkness.

"Oh!" She gave a little cry of dismay.

"It's all right. The usual thing." Blake hunted around in his right jacket pocket and withdrew a small torch, flicking it on. "Now's the time to tell me you've got your emergency kit in hand."

It was good to say yes. "I might have known this was going to happen."

"You mean you somehow worked it the tree fell across the road?"

She knew he was taunting her, yet keyed up as she was, she answered quietly. "I'd never do anything to put you in danger."

"I've decided you do, whether you want to or not."

Carrie walked away rapidly, and Blake followed her. In the kitchen she seized the kit and set it on the table. It contained medical supplies, torches, new batteries, candles, an oil lamp, tins of food, an opener and a change of clothes for her and her father.

Blake got the lamp going, and the room was filled with a mellow, golden light that didn't reach into the shadowy recesses.

"Better get out of those damp clothes," he ordered crisply. "But get fully dressed again. Lord knows what we can expect tonight."

He's not talking about the cyclone, either, Carrie thought, acutely tuned to his wavelength. "What about you?" she asked with concern, her eyes moving over his tall body. She loved looking at it. The wide, straight set of his shoulders, narrow waist, lean hips, the long length of his legs.

"Don't worry about me," he said with the faintest impatience. "I'll just take off this jacket. My raincoat was immeasurably more effective than yours."

"I'm not surprised. Mine has most of the studs missing."

"I'll get you a new one," he said tersely.

"Are you angry with me, Blake?" she asked hesitantly. "Angry you're forced to stay here?"

He glanced at her briefly, blue eyes dark. "Don't be absurd. I've got a few concerns, that's all." He handed her a candlestick, watched her stare into the flickering flame. "Scared to go by yourself?"

"Not a bit," she said staunchly. "You can pull me back if I'm blown out a window."

"That's what I'm here for, Carolyn," he said.

In the bedroom Carrie moved swiftly, pulling out fresh clothes. With the storm shutters closed, the air was damp and sticky with heat. Normally the ceiling fans would be working full blast, but not without electricity. She settled on a sleeveless cotton shirt and shorts. It was much too hot for anything else. Even the pink shirt she tied at the midriff, instead of tucking it in. Dry sneakers went on her feet. Her hair was towelled and piled high, letting long, glowing strands fall where they wanted.

When she returned to the kitchen Blake had set the table for a light meal. "Better have something to eat," he said in a business-like tone then lifted his gaze. It moved slowly over her face and body and down her long, gleaming legs. "Couldn't you have picked something a little less tantalising?" he asked, his voice rasping.

She turned up a confused face. "I haven't made the slightest attempt to make myself tantalising."

"You expect me to believe that?"

She flushed under his mocking gaze. "Blake, *please*. It's so hot, this outfit makes sense."

"You don't have to account to *me*," he said with black humour. "On the other hand, you've put spells on me before."

"Not that *I* can recall," Carrie retorted quickly.

"Really!" His blue eyes were electric. "I thought you ravishing at the country club dinner-dance."

"And here *I* was thinking your whole attention was focused on Diane." She knew as soon as she said it it was the wrong thing.

There was a fraught silence, then Blake answered very crisply. "Now that's a damned silly remark if ever I've heard one."

"Is it?" She lifted her softly cleft chin.

"Yes, it is. I take exception to that little gibe."

"Then I'll say no more about it." She moved further into the room. "You've done a good job of setting the table. What are we going to have?" She walked a little hesitantly towards the refrigerator, not surprised when Blake didn't move out of her way. Tall herself, he made her feel small.

"So nervy?" The lamplight gleamed off his eyes, his dark polished skin and high cheekbones, accentuated the cool sensuality of his mouth.

"Why not? You're deliberately trying to rattle me."

"Oh, come on! Be honest for once."

"All right! It's this damned cyclone. The wind and the rain. The *heat*. It makes me crazy. And you can take that maddening smile off your mouth," she added a little wildly.

Immediately he straightened. "I'm sorry," he said tightly. "You're under a lot of strain."

"And don't be nice to me, either."

"So I'll move right up to the end of the table. How's that?"

She made a helpless little gesture of conciliation. "Don't take any notice of me, Blake, I know I'm off balance."

"Not surprising. I don't want to take advantage of it, either."

Several times during the meal Blake got up to check around the house. Built to withstand cyclones, it nevertheless was moaning and groaning like some great animate creature in pain.

"I suppose you didn't have that section over the bathroom fixed?" he asked after his last trip.

Carrie hung her head. "Actually, no."

"The roof could come off," he told her bluntly.

"Do you think I haven't considered that?"

A flash of something like anger crossed his face. "We'll just have to start praying, I guess."

"Lord knows what Dad does with the money," Carrie said by way of apology.

"You do what you can, Carolyn. I don't mean to blame you in any way. There are far too many trees surrounding the house. With all the leaves, the guttering can't take the volume of water." He reached for the battery-operated radio. "Let's see if we can get something else. Even if the cyclone passes over the Rainbow Bay area, we're going to feel it hard."

Carrie pressed her fingers over her eyes. "You should be at Courtland Downs where you belong." Her voice was husky with worry and slipping control. "What if something goes wrong?"

"I've got people to take care of it. I'm here with *you*. That's the way of it."

All they got from the radio was a whole lot of static and a disembodied voice. Carrie began to clear away, and afterwards they took the lamp and a couple of candlesticks into the living room.

The drumming of the rain on the roof was deafening, with sudden violent assaults on the shutters as though the wind was a malevolent beast determined to enter. It was harrowing in the extreme. Without Blake, Carrie thought she would be very frightened indeed. As it was, her body was filled with peculiar tensions. A primitive awareness of the elemental things in life.

She was lying full length on the sofa. It was impossible to sleep. She was almost sick with the heat and the clamourings within her. The house sounded like it was about to break up. Blake lolled in an armchair opposite her, his dark head tilted back, but he was far from relaxed. When he spoke she caught the flash of his white teeth and the curious jewel-like shimmer of his eyes. Both of them were like coiled animals in a cage. Both on a leash, each intensely aware of the other.

Around two o'clock the eye of the cyclone produced a temporary lull that was even more ominous than the driving rain and high winds.

Carrie, dozing fitfully on the sofa, gave an odd little whimper and sat up in panic. Where was Blake? She drew in her breath sharply and stood at the precise moment the winds returned, with ferocity. They crashed against the front of the house, which seemed to move on its stumps. A pair of shutters blew out, and the wind, triumphant, came howling and rushing at her. Something lifted. An ornament. It hit her. The next second Blake had her hard around the waist, drawing her swiftly backwards towards the kitchen, the strongest part of the house. Without wasting a second, he shoved the heavy old cedar table against the wall, pushing her under it. She touched her arm, feeling the stickiness of blood. The broken ornament had cut her, and she hadn't even felt it. Blake, too, lowered himself to the floor, too tall to attempt to seek protection under the heavy table.

Carrie must have put out her hand, because he took it and kept it in his own. They could hear the wind prowling through the rooms, its breath whistling like a train. It was looking for them. She was almost sure of it. Another shutter blew loose. Next they heard the sound of shattering glass, like a series of pistol shots. Carrie let her head fall between her knees. Would they even *have* a house when this was over? From somewhere near the bedrooms came a terrible splitting sound, then a crack. Blake got up, hell-bent on finding out what it was.

"Stay here, Blake," she shouted, perched on the fine edge of panic. What if anything happened to him? To Blake Courtland. It was unthinkable. She nerved herself to scramble out from under the table and go after him even when he yelled at her to stay back.

In the hallway he caught her to him, arresting her flight. His voice was so loud, so commanding it rang in her ears. "Stay put. You can't help me."

"You stay put, too." She wasn't aware of it, but she was clinging to him as though she would never let him go. "I can take anything but your getting hurt."

"I'm not going to get hurt." He was indifferent to the dangers, steadily easing her against the wall. "God," he muttered. "There's a gash in your arm. Blood. Why didn't you tell me?"

"I can't feel it. Don't worry." She shook her head.

"I'll need to look at it." He cursed as a violent gust of wind inside the house sent more objects spinning. "Stay here for just a few minutes," he exhorted her, his strong hands biting into her shoulders. "I have to check out that noise."

"Then be careful." She didn't try to stop him this time, and her voice was too faint to be heard.

At some stage Carrie became aware the battering force of the wind had somewhat abated, although torrents of rain continued to pour down. This side of the house was so *dark*. She didn't see Blake until he was almost on her, reaching out and enclosing her in his protective arms.

"We're going to ride it out." He sounded almost elated. "The bathroom has taken the worst of it. A tree's down. Branches have crashed right through the window. It can be all cleaned up. I've shut the door and bagged it. Come back to the kitchen, Carolyn. That arm needs attention."

For a moment, as he cleaned and dressed it, Carrie felt a touch of giddiness.

"You okay?"

The crispness of his tone steadied her.

"I'm fine." There was a touching note of stoicism in her husky reply. "One of these days I'm going to thank you properly for everything you do."

He gave her a taut smile. "One thing you *can* do is stay put when I tell you to."

"I know. You're a bossy man."

"And you're not good at taking orders."

"I was worried about you, Blake."

"That's exactly what I like to hear." His blue eyes touched on her pale face, sensing the sadness that was in her. "Now what if you lie down for a while?"

She shook her head. "I couldn't sleep."

"Maybe not. But you're very pale, and that gash is fairly deep. What about a couple of pain-killers?"

She nodded. The wound was throbbing. "There are some in the cupboard just behind you."

He found the bottle, shook two tablets into her hand, turned to get a glass of water from the tap. The water burst through the pipes, and Blake drew back involuntarily. "To hell with that," he said shortly, adjusting the pressure.

Carrie drank thirstily. Nothing was as good as water at the right time. Her mouth was dry. Every nerve in her body was stretched tight.

"Come along, Carolyn," Blake said with exquisite gentleness, yet in her overwrought state she found it violently erotic.

He reached out to assist her but she recoiled, more out of fear of revealing her own blinding need than anything else.

"You have nothing to fear," he told her harshly, reacting to her agitated withdrawal, her almost palpable air of panic.

"I'm sorry. You startled me." She tried desperately to apologize.

"I wasn't about to drag you off to your bedroom," he said with sharp disgust.

"I said I'm sorry, Blake." Her green eyes were huge, penitent. "I overreacted."

"I don't believe that," he returned curtly. "I *can't*. Some kind of fear dictates all your actions. But you can't bring yourself to admit it."

"It's only because I must do what's best."

"Then why sound so broken-hearted?" His tone mocked her.

"I can't *control* it." With an effort she moved, trying to conquer the pressure that was growing, wave upon wave, inside her. His handsome face swam before her eyes. The room was filled with turbulence.

"Oh, goddamn," he moaned, sounding as though he, too, was at the end of his tether. "Carolyn, *talk* to me." Her long hair had blown forward all around her face, and he all but snatched it away.

"Not tonight, Blake. I *can't*." All her energy had seeped away with the force of the tempest, his extraordinary power over her.

"You're impossible," he said with an element of exhaustion. "I don't know how long I can put up with it."

Her large green eyes filled with tears. "Then there's no need to be with me at all."

"It so happens I *want* to be. Now there's a sick joke. I thought I *knew* you, Carolyn. Have I been wrong all along?"

"I can't do everything you want, Blake." She blinked furiously, trying all of a sudden to move past him. *I can't let you look inside me,* she thought wildly.

"So tell me, what is it I want? As you see it," he asked in hard challenge. "Some kind of affair? Some secret passion? Little Carrie Donovan as my mistress?"

"Why not?" She flung up her glowing head, as though charged by electricity. "I'm not Diane Anthony. I can't take my place in your world quite so easily."

His blue eyes flared like kindling thrown on a flame. "I don't believe this," he said in a voice that was hard-edged with anger. "I hope and pray, Carolyn, that I've always approached you with respect."

Of course, it was true. What demon was driving her? "So I'm putting it all wrongly," she cried. "I'm sick and frightened. Can't you hear all that furore outside?"

"Be damned with it." His vibrant voice was ragged at the edges. "I can hear your heart knocking louder. Why don't we get this over? Then I'll leave you alone. It's what you seem to want."

While she stood unresistant, trapped by her own deep desires, he reached for her, wrapping his arm tightly around her waist and drawing her close against the taut strength of his body.

"I've waited *years* to kiss you." His voice was a low, exciting growl. "It's time enough."

At the first touch of his mouth, Carrie's excitation was so great she thought her legs would give under her.

He must have thought so, too, because his hard hold increased, locking her to him as though there was nowhere else she could possibly go.

It was a masterpiece of male power, of wild confrontation, a moment she had been waiting for all the days of her life. He kissed her over and over, deep, insistent, all-consuming kisses that made the blood glitter in her veins. Time seemed to be standing still, yet it was racing, every second supercharged with passion. She desperately needed his hands on her body. But if he touched her, nothing would ever be the same again. Such was his powerful hold on her, she felt she could agree to whatever he wanted.

His hands began to caress her, deepening the beats of rapture, sending great, shuddering ripples deep into her body. He made love like he did everything else. With such mastery. Yet she felt she was matching him. They were like two splendid creatures of the wild running swiftly, effortlessly side by side. As his hands cupped her breasts she felt a flaring ecstasy mixed up with a tearing panic. It was an instinctual thing, telling her passion was extravagant, costly, dangerous. It had to be paid for. Her involuntary cry was muffled by the deep, warm pressure of his mouth.

"Blake!"

She had become lost to him. The reality of his lovemaking was far, far more tumultuous than she had ever dreamed or imagined. Every inch of her skin glowed with heat.

"I'm here." He lifted his head almost languorously, brushing back the hair that was billowing richly around her face.

"Do you know what you do to me?"

"Whatever it is, I'm glad."

"I never dreamed," she murmured, lifting unsteady fingers to touch his mouth. The mouth she loved.

"What it would be like?"

She nodded, and a moment later lowered her head onto his shoulder as though spent. Her heart was fluttering wildly in her breast, her body and mind in a kind of delirium.

"I think I've always known," he said in a low voice that still vibrated through her. "You're perfect to make love to."

He didn't release her, and she clung to him still, the depths of her sexuality much greater than she'd ever thought. Even the fury of the night was transformed. It was a fitting background for the tempestuous spirit of their lovemaking. The house was empty. There was no one to know. No one to see. But Blake's sense of honour overcame his scorching desire.

With a final hard kiss he set her free. His fingers redid the few buttons of her shirt, even then lingering against the soft lustre of her flesh. "This might be the most selfless thing I've ever done," he said wryly. "God knows I'm risking it, but I'd never abuse your trust."

"I know. Even when I can scarcely move. I'm not even trying to."

"Carolyn!" He shook his head as though to summon up extra self-control from some deep inner reservoir.

"I can't," she whispered. It was true. No luring game.

"You've got to. You might think you know what desire is like, but I'm a starved man."

"You shouldn't be. You could have anyone."

He swept her with his dazzling eyes. "I didn't say I wanted anyone. I want you."

That was something she could no longer doubt. But in what role? Overwhelming as it was, passion wasn't love. Nor a lasting commitment.

CHAPTER THREE

SHE woke to the sound of rain and a bedroom filled with a soft, grey mist, a combination of damp and humidity. Her eyelids fluttered. Memories of the night before flooded back with great clarity, causing a sudden rush of blood to her skin. She felt such an aching warmth it was almost as though Blake was beside her. She could feel the strength of his body, the touch of his mouth and hands, inhale the scent of him that reminded her of lustrous veneers and fine leather. The currents that had long flowed between them had finally surged together.

At some point after she had fallen asleep he must have come back, because a light rug lay across her legs. Gently she pushed it aside and went to the door. There was no sound at all in the house. Moments later she found Blake's note propped up on the kitchen table. She picked it up, delighting in his beautiful handwriting. Confident, flowing, quintessentially masculine. Phone and electricity had been restored, he told her. He had checked with Courtland Downs. Everything was under control. The tree had been removed from the road at Bangara. He would contact her during some part of the morning. He concluded with a single riveting line. "It was *no* dream."

Indeed it wasn't. No dream could come even close to reality. Carrie folded the note and put it in her pocket. At some stage, she thought, she might frame it. Outside the rain was still coming down, but without the terrifying force of the day before. It wasn't lashing the house or coming onto the veranda. Blake had found time to open the shutters. Cooling air was flowing through the rooms. On further investigation she discovered he had removed the branches that were coming through the bathroom window, hanging a tarpaulin outside.

The garden was flattened, the grass a thick sea of coloured petals and blossoms. One of the young tulip trees was down, and a side fence covered in a rampant white bougainvillea lay on the ground. In the distance the plantation looked as sturdy as ever, even if the balance of the crop had been ruined.

In the hallway she rang the hospital to check on her father, only to be told to hold on. Eventually her father's doctor came to the phone and told her in a near angry tone her father had discharged himself.

"A law unto himself, is Mick," he said sternly. "Once we got him out of pain, that was it. We did manage to take a few blood samples and an ultrasound. No results as yet. Too many other things going on with the cyclone. It's all going to come against him one day, Carrie. With a vengeance," he added. Carrie, long used to her father, could only agree.

At nine o'clock her father arrived home. He had cadged a ride with an emergency crew who stayed long enough to reinforce the section of roofing over the bathroom area.

"All you had to do, Dad, was stay for a day or two," Carrie pointed out as she made her father a cup of tea. "We can't use the hospital when we feel like it, then simply walk out. Dr. Richards was quite angry."

"He would be," Michael Donovan acknowledged, "but I don't have to do every blessed thing he wants. He seems to think I passed the stone, but he wanted me to have an endoscope or something. I can't remember."

"But Dad, you wouldn't *feel* it, and you're so brave."

"Not with things shoved down my throat I'm not," her father said, and yawned. "Besides, I was worried about you. You must have had a bad night."

Carrie hesitated only briefly. "It *was* scary, but it could have been a whole lot worse. I could have been alone. Blake had to stay—a tree came down across the road at Bangara Crossing."

"Well, well, well," Michael Donovan said, raising his eyes to look directly at his daughter. "Are you sure Blake didn't organise it?"

"Oh, Dad!" Carrie moved away.

"Don't oh, Dad me!" Michael Donovan answered promptly. "Blake's as good an organiser as ever I've seen, and that includes my army days. I'd say he's been waiting years to get you alone."

"Have fun," Carrie said.

"It's true!"

"He doesn't have the reputation for being a man of integrity for nothing."

"You mean he didn't even try to kiss you?" Michael Donovan looked at his daughter in open disbelief.

"Just a pleasant peck good night." Lord! she thought.

"I find it very difficult to credit that. You're attracted to him, aren't you?"

Carrie hesitated and then acknowledged it wryly. "Exceedingly so."

"Ah, well, I know your mother would approve, and Blake and I get on well together," her father said after a moment's serious reflection.

"He hasn't offered to *marry* me, Dad."

"Don't be surprised if he's considering it," Michael Donovan said and rolled his eyes heavenward. "I've been observing the man closely. He'll have a beautiful wife, healthy children, and you'll have all the money you want."

"Money's not a big deal." Carrie looked at her father seriously.

"Of *course* it is!" Michael Donovan jeered. "Besides, someone's got to look after your old man."

"It would make sense if my father started looking after *himself*," Carrie said, and bent to kiss him on the head.

It wasn't until late afternoon Blake arrived, bone tired after a long, hard day in the saddle shifting cattle to higher ground. Like Carrie, he was perturbed at Michael Donovan's defection from hospital but not surprised.

"Think about it, Mick, the next time they might refuse to treat you."

"Ah, don't be angry with me, Blake." Michael Donovan tried unsuccessfully to turn on the charm. "I'd like to pick my own time to have an operation. *If* I need one. Meanwhile, I promise you I'll take better care of myself."

"I'd like to believe it," Blake said to Carrie as he was leaving some time later. "Unfortunately for my peace of mind, I can't." His tone was tight.

"Anyway he's looking better," Carrie managed to say, acutely aware of Blake's tension.

"The thing is, Carolyn, *you* deserve a better life." Abruptly he took hold of her chin and dropped a hard kiss on her mouth. "Ring me if you need me. At any time. It doesn't matter."

"Blake?" She was loath to ask more of him.

"I need to know." His voice conveyed concern and anger.

"Then I promise I'll call."

Three nights later, with the rain still falling and the roads slippery and dangerous, Michael Donovan alarmed Carrie by saying he was going into town.

"What for, Dad?" She jumped up. "Can't it wait until morning?"

"No, it *can't*," Michael Donovan said in a voice intolerant of opposition. "I need to see Sandy. He's not a well man, as you know."

"It seems to me he'd feel a whole lot better if he stopped drinking so heavily," Carrie pointed out.

Her father turned angrily to face her. "You ought to remember he's a victim of war, girl. Sandy was *tortured*."

"And you got him out. I know, Dad. I'm very sorry for all your tragic experiences. But the nightmare's over. You and Sandy have to survive."

"What would *you* know about the horror buried inside of us?" Michael Donovan asked in a bitter, morose voice. "Your generation have been spared, thank God. Only the ones who've been through it know."

"Then take care, Dad," Carrie said wearily. It was useless to argue any further.

Left on her own, Carrie began to think. It was high time she made a life for herself. Blake was right, after all. The twins had their careers. They were on course to become surgeons. No matter how hard she tried to help her father, he went determinedly on his way. Surely she was entitled to a life of her own after all the years of sacrifice?

As for Blake... Whatever his interest in her, and neither of them could deny a strong attraction at heart, she felt she was reaching for the stars.

Attraction didn't always lead to the altar, just like a fairy story. Amanda's death had left Blake in the kind of emotional limbo she knew so well. Now he was out of it, but there was still Diane. Denied Blake when her sister was alive, Diane was still very much part of his life and determined to stay there. The families remained close. Devoted to one another and their way of life. The past and the future yet to come together. Absolutely nothing was certain. Nothing.

She ate a ham sandwich for supper and continued working through the evening, waiting to hear the sound of the four-wheel drive coming up the drive. Shortly after ten a vehicle turned into the drive, coming to a halt at the base of the front steps. The exterior lights were on, and as she pulled back the curtains in the living room she recognised Blake's Range Rover. Anxiety flooded her. Something had to be wrong. She lived constantly with the terrible worry one night her father might fall asleep at the wheel and run off the road. Carrie flew to the front door, throwing it open only to see Blake supporting her father up the stairs.

"Is he all right?" she called, her initial fright suddenly turning to anger.

Michael Donovan managed to raise his head. "Don't go on now, Carrie. There's a good girl."

She could hear the drink in his voice, and she burned with humiliation. Why did he do this to himself? To her? It was so demeaning.

Blake knew the layout of the house. Still supporting her father, he made towards the bedroom.

"Blathering drunk I am," Michael Donovan told her unnecessarily. "Like a fool I let Sandy take me off to the pub."

"Sandy's the fool!" Carrie moved swiftly, folding back the quilt and turning the bed down. "Does he want you to wind up in hospital after a terrible accident?"

"Let it be, Carrie," her father groaned. "Sandy's a friend of mine. I don't need you to worry your head off about me."

How could she not? Carrie moved into the hallway where she pulled a couple of towels out of the built-in cupboard. When she returned to the bedroom Blake had her father lying comfortably on the bed.

"You're hair's wet, Dad." Ignoring her father's protests, she towelled his face and head. She should have known he would only go into town to get himself drunk.

"That's enough, Carolyn," Blake said almost sternly. "Let your father sleep it off."

In fact Michael Donovan had already closed his eyes in merciful oblivion.

"I can't protect him. I *can't*." Carrie felt sickness and upset in the pit of her stomach. Why had Blake to be around to witness all this?

"Your father's a grown man. You can't live his life for him. Let's go into another room."

Carrie moved blindly, striving for self-control.

"How did you manage to meet up with him?" She turned, her face flushed, her eyes over-bright. "*Please* don't tell me he was reeling in the streets."

With one flowing motion Blake drew her into the living room. "I got a message from a mutual friend to the effect Mick had had too much to drink."

"I begged him not to go into town," Carrie said wretchedly. "But he must see Sandy. You know how Sandy leans on him."

"They forged that bond in Vietnam, Carolyn. It can't be broken."

"It's hell, Blake." She whirled tempestuously. "Dad saved Sandy's life. Sandy is going to get Dad *killed*."

"There is that fear." His expression darkened. "You're shaking."

"I'm so *angry*." To her horror, her eyes filled with tears. "Why are you always there for us?"

"Why do you always have to sound like you bitterly resent it?"

"Because I *do*." Every nerve was aquiver with grief, pain, intense humiliation.

"Then you shouldn't," Blake told her bluntly. "What are friends for if you can't turn to them? Do you want me to go?"

"Yes." At that moment she saw no other way. It took courage to turn to him in such an intensely emotional state. "For all you say, the gap between us is all too real. Surely you can see it now. You're always having to come to my rescue. And it is me, isn't it?"

"I don't trouble to deny it." His eyes took her in, the rich flowing hair, her distinctive face so full of emotion, the fine line of her throat, the delicate set of her shoulders, the slopes of her breasts. "I'm growing impatient now of everything that comes between us."

"You're too grand for me, Blake. For *us*," she told him in some anguish.

"Don't talk such utter rubbish. No one can take your dignity from you. You can't claim responsibility for your father's actions. Besides, there are compelling reasons for Mick's problems."

"I know that. But you don't have to get mixed up in them. You have a position to maintain. A public life. Forgive me if I ask, but what role has Diane Anthony to play in it? She's a young woman of privilege. She comes from a distinguished family. You're still very close."

Blake's brilliant eyes turned cold. "Why look at me so accusingly? I haven't deceived you about anything. Diane is Amanda's sister."

"And you were very much in love with Amanda. You'd be happily married by now."

"But it didn't happen like that, did it? So why bring it up? And why now? I'll always remember Amanda. But she's a memory. Life goes on."

"But you're involving me in this now. Turning my world upside down. Can't I ask if Diane has become more to you than a friend?"

His expression was tough and unemotional. "Diane remains what she's always been."

Carrie's green eyes flashed challenge. "I find it difficult to accept that."

"Really?" He shrugged. "Is there something you know I don't? You must tell me."

"Very simply, she told me."

"Of course. Women. To hell with the lot of you." He swung away in disgust.

Carrie took a deep breath and went after him. "Is it a lie?" She grasped his arm, losing herself for a moment in the turbulent blue of his eyes.

"And you very much want to know?" He stared down his straight, arrogant nose at her.

The quick temper of the redhead was flashing to the surface. "I seem to remember you kissing me passionately."

"And you loved it. Right?"

"I didn't have all that much say in the matter." It was a pathetic taunt, but somehow it worked.

"Actually you got exactly what you begged for. And you're getting more." Steely hands skimmed her slender hips, circled her waist, moved up to her rib cage, tightened just beneath her breasts.

"You *know*, damn you," he muttered, lowering his dark head. "You know how much I want you." Overcome by his own urgency, he caught up her mouth, claiming it with a hard male passion. It was like some fevered love dance with Carrie arching back in futile resistance and Blake propelling her closer and closer into his arms.

Finally the excitement was too much for her. She gave herself up to it. To him. Allowing him to kiss her so deeply, so voluptuously, she had that powerful sensation again. They were running freely across a giant landscape, filled with incredibly beautiful sights and sounds.

There were clouds of rose, gold and white billowing across the celestial blue sky, wonderful animals everywhere, mythical creatures, unicorns, their horned foreheads set with jewels, silky winged butterflies of glorious colour and size sailing about them. Flowers unfurled one after the other, flowers with giant petals, releasing their perfume into the warm, golden air. They were running in a dream. It was paradise, rapturous. She couldn't believe in her own happiness.

When finally Blake released her she gave a sharp little cry of withdrawal, but he only looked at her in a hard, disturbing way as though reinforcing the power of the male over the female.

"Understand now," he said, very clearly and deliberately, "if you've never understood before. I need you. And I'm going to get you. I don't expect to hear any more nonsense about my being too grand. Whatever *that* might be. I'm a man like any other. In any case, you take some living up to yourself. No more talk about Diane and her position in my life, either. It's *you* I want. Have you got it?"

There was a hard edge to the way he was speaking, almost a lick of violence in the dazzling blue of his gaze, but Carrie, looking up, caught her image at the very centre of his eyes.

CHAPTER FOUR

THAT night marked the turning point in Carrie's life. When Blake had to fly to the state capital two days later for a series of important meetings, he told Carrie in advance of his plans, assuring her he would be home in time for the annual post-harvest dinner-dance, one of the social highlights of the year. It was to be held in the handsome new town community centre, heavily subsidized by Courtland money.

"It's about time the town saw us together," he said firmly.

Her father, coming in for lunch, could hardly fail to notice the stars in his daughter's eyes.

"The wonderful Blake Courtland, I take it. He's rung?"

Carrie turned to him, hands outstretched. "He's asked me to the harvest dinner-dance."

"Coming courting, is he?" Michael Donovan smiled laconically. "Your mother would have been thrilled out of her mind. Doted on him like a son. Thought he was perfect, which I'd have to say he is. Or as perfect as mortal man gets. You'll have to get yourself a new dress, shoes, the works. I want you to do us proud. You can bet your life Miss Diane Anthony will have her snooty nose out of joint."

"Will she ever." Carrie sobered abruptly at the thought. "I wish you'd change your mind and come with us, Dad."

Michael Donovan shook his head. "Too many memories, love. Your mother and I always had a marvellous time together. You go along and enjoy yourself for both of us.''

On that particular Saturday evening, when Carrie was finished dressing, she went into the living room to get her father's opinion.

He set the paper aside and rose to his feet.

''Beautiful!'' he said, his eyes filling unashamedly with tears.

Carrie couldn't answer for a moment, moved by her father's emotion. ''I worked hard at it, Dad, I can tell you.''

''Why, you look like an art nouveau figure my grandmother used to have. Girl into flower. An arum lily or some such thing. It was a lovely piece. The only tiny reservation I have is—''

''It shows more of me than I usually show,'' Carrie finished off for him. ''It's evening, Dad.''

''God help poor Blake!'' her father mumbled. ''I'll be here when he drops you off. Don't you worry about that. Perhaps I should ask his intentions.''

''Don't you dare!'' Carrie went to him, kissed his cheek, then began dancing around the room. The dress she was wearing was in the twenties style, a deceptively simple, superbly cut slip that demanded a nymph's body inside it. The colour was Nile green, the fabric a beautiful silk chiffon. The ankle length showed off her elegant, colour-matched evening pumps. The effect was romantic, innocent, sexy all at the same time. Tonight her hair was indeed her crowning glory, spilling down her back but dressed up and away from her face. She wore no jewellery other than three silver bangles studded with opals and a pair of silver and enamel antique drop earrings, favourite pieces that had belonged to her mother.

''Miraculous!'' her father stated, sounding both proud and sad. ''I just know your mother can see you.''

"Of course she can, Dad." Carrie broke off her dancing, her silk-banded skirt floating back into line.

Blake arrived less than ten minutes later, looking stunning in his evening clothes. Tonight he wore a summer white dinner jacket with a red carnation in his lapel, his whole aura exuding money, power, style. Beside him James Bond might look drab, Carrie thought. Her heart gave a painful lurch. This wasn't one of those little inner ecstasies she often had. It was *real*. Still the feeling persisted—in another minute she would wake up, back in her working clothes like Cinderella.

The community centre was almost filled when they arrived, the huge space humming with music, conversation, laughter. In a climate committed to casual, everyone went all out for special occasions. The North was prosperous. Sugar was booming, tea, coffee, tropical fruits, tourism and cattle production. Many of the established families, as well as the entrepreneur newcomers, were very rich indeed.

Carrie had paid hundreds of dollars for her dress, but she knew many of the other women's dresses had cost thousands. She recognised a flowered silk Versace on the glamorous Italian wife of a well-known land developer who sometimes went into partnership with Courtland Enterprises.

If people were surprised to see her on Blake's arm, most only registered pleasure. As Blake's partner, Carrie found herself automatically at the official table, but when the superb four-course dinner was over the young men of the district wasted no time in claiming dances.

Blake appeared to find it irritating from time to time, but in any event he had to entertain the mayor's house guest, a forceful, rather humourless woman politician with an agenda of her own.

"Hoping everyone will vote for her at the next election," Tim McConnell, her long-time admirer, said,

his arm closing possessively around Carrie. "Blake didn't
seem too happy giving you up. How come he got to ask
you tonight? That's quite a coup."

"I guess he likes me," Carrie said with some emphasis.

Tim snorted. "Hey, who wouldn't? Men don't just
like girls like you, Carrie. They fall in love with them.
I've never seen you looking so ravishing. That dress is
a dream. Springtime. Flowers. Maybe you'd better not
look around. Diane is dancing with dear Jonathan!
They're right behind us. The look on *her* face would
make you wilt." He lowered his voice. "It's really weird,
her wearing her hair like Amanda, don't you think? At
a distance you'd swear it *was* Amanda. Blake wouldn't
want that kind of reminder. Bad enough living with a
tragedy. I suppose she's using her resemblance to
Amanda to stay close to Blake."

"I'd say you've hit it right on the head. Can we stop
talking about the Anthonys?"

"Sure." Tim shrugged but continued anyway. "I know
Diane expects to make a match of it. That's the betting,
anyway. But she wouldn't be any comfort to him. She's
as self-centred as they come."

"Blake might realise that. He's with *me*."

"For now, anyway. But the super rich usually stick to
their own kind." Tim looked at her mournfully. "I was
praying his eye wouldn't fall on you, but it figures it
would. What did he actually *say*?"

"What on earth do you mean?" Carrie drew back.

"Well, what does he want? A relationship? A bit of
a fling? You're beautiful, you know, though you don't
seem too aware of it."

"He may want excitement, risk," Carrie answered in
a brittle voice.

"You're joking." Tim sucked in his breath.

"That's what you're implying."

"Well, can he be serious about you? Apart from anything else, he's so damned rich, a big man in the state, and he must be a good ten years older than you."

"Nine," Carrie corrected, thinking this was only the beginning of the opposition. "Are you calling him staid?"

"Staid? Good grief! If he wanted you it would be like trying to stop an avalanche. Don't get in too deep, that's all. Beside Blake you're just a baby. You could get badly hurt."

When Tim returned Carrie to her table Blake rose to his impressive six foot three. "You'll excuse me, Mrs. Miller." He glanced down at the politician. "I'm like the rest of the men around here. I want a dance with Carolyn."

"I hope you'll have a chance to dance with *me*," the woman replied in such a flirtatious way, it confounded them all.

On the dance floor Carrie looked over Blake's shoulder. "You've made a conquest there."

"Don't blame me. I'm just doing my job. Actually I've been extremely patient with her—and your legion of admirers. It's my turn to enjoy myself. Come closer to me, Carolyn. How does that feel?" His every movement was fluid, effortless. He made her feel like a traveller in paradise.

"Fabulous, but *everyone* is looking at us."

"Let them. They'd be looking at you whoever you were with. You look wonderful in that dress. You should never take it off."

"Thank you." She flushed a little under his blue gaze. "Not the thing to do the pruning in, though."

"Leave the pruning to the men," Blake advised, giving a quick frown. "Surely you're not handling the saw?"

"Why not?"

"You might live a lot longer if you don't. If you *must* prune, do it by hand. But let's leave plantation business for tonight." Blake sighed. "I want you to enjoy yourself. No more dancing with Tim McConnell, either. I can't stand his fool drooling."

Wonderful as it was, it was impossible to stay together. Blake had his own determined following. Carrie had hers. As a community occasion, it was expected partners wouldn't remain exclusively together. It was well after midnight when Carrie thought she should show a little initiative and go in search of Blake. Her confidence was up. The district had seen her by Blake's side. It was all going down rather well. Of course, there had been a few searching questions, from Tim mostly, and friends of the Anthonys. She had to expect that. And deal with it.

Blake didn't appear to be anywhere inside the hall. Perhaps he had gone outside for a breath of fresh air. Maybe even to escape. As the evening had worn on, the woman politician had undergone an incredible sea change, looking at Blake through half-closed eyes. She had even returned from the powder room with her abundant blond hair combed out of its French pleat and swinging wildly around her shoulders in an absolute kicking over of the traces.

Outside in the tropical night the sky was lit by a great languorous copper moon. It drenched the lawns and gardens in a golden radiance, but there were areas where the tree ferns and golden canes formed dark perfumed arbours. The frangipani, the oleanders, the tuberoses and gardenias were heavily in bloom, their delicious fragrance spiking the warm air. Quite a few couples were strolling arm in arm. Others were seated on the stairs or dancing on the lawn. Just as Carrie decided Blake had to be somewhere inside, she caught the sound of Diane Anthony's voice from somewhere in the shadows.

The tone was agonized, betrayed. "But you let me think—"

Carrie stood riveted, waiting for the answer. It came. As she knew it would.

"*What*, Diane?" It was Blake, his tone hard, even brutal.

"You care for me. You know you do. There's been no one since Amanda. It's upset me dreadfully to see you with that Donovan girl. How *could* you ask her when you know perfectly well I was expecting to be your partner?"

"Oh, come, Diane. Have you the right to expect that?"

"Yes!" Diane's answer carried a wealth of conviction. "You *gave* me the right. I've been in your company constantly for years. You loved Amanda, yet you betray her memory with someone like Carrie Donovan. Who *is* she, I ask you? Her mother might have been acceptable, but her father's the town drunk."

Carrie shut her eyes in the darkness, her heart moving in pain. The town drunk. My God! Was that the best one could say of a war hero?

There was a short silence, then Diane continued. "I'm sorry. *Sorry.*" She sounded contrite, chastened. "I know he's had his tragedy, as we have, but she's not the right girl for you. How could she be? She's beautiful, I grant you. She speaks well, but she could never take Amanda's place at your side. She simply doesn't have the background. She couldn't be *less* like Amanda. It's *we* who have that common bond. You told me once, remember? Amanda was our common bond."

"Evidently you misinterpreted it." Blake sounded grim.

"I don't think so." Diane was vehement in her denial. "You're cruel, Blake. So cruel. Under the charm is a dark side. In some ways you're a tyrant. You've kept me chained to you. You've allowed me to believe—''

Carrie's head was spinning. She put her hands over her ears. Blake and Diane, when he'd *denied* it. Suddenly the whole situation seemed intolerable. Ill-conceived. She wanted no part of it. She turned away swiftly, her pleasure in the evening totally spoiled.

Her change of mood wasn't lost on Blake. She was conscious he watched her for the rest of the night, his brilliant blue eyes hooded. On the way home he stopped the car in a viewing bay overlooking the shimmering water. The moon had laid down a golden track across the surface, so seemingly substantial one might have thought to walk on it.

"So what's wrong?" Blake asked her in a quiet voice.

Carrie tried desperately to salvage her pride. "Really, nothing's the matter. I've had a wonderful night."

"I thought you did, up to a point. Would you like to go for a walk on the beach?"

"I don't think so, Blake. It's very late."

"Should that bother us? We're both over twenty-one. Leave your shoes in the car."

"I'd only ruin my stockings."

"I'll buy you another pair," he answered rather tersely. He came around to the passenger side to let her out. "Until we're on the soft sand I'll carry you."

"That's not necessary, Blake. Not at all."

"Why deprive me of the pleasure?" He lifted her regardless, cradling her in the starry dark.

"Takes what he wants. Does what he wants," Carrie chanted in a sad, off-key voice.

"Do you object?"

"Perhaps I should. Sometimes I feel like a woman on the edge. The *very* edge."

"And how are you feeling *now*?"

"Losing it," she murmured, feeling the urgent pressure of wanting him. Her enslavement had begun.

He gave a short answering laugh and began to move down the slope. "You couldn't have been more poised and confident tonight. I had a terrible urge to warn all your admirers off. Especially McConnell. In case you haven't noticed, he hasn't got too much between the ears."

"Certainly he does."

He lowered her to the sand, holding her lightly with one arm. "I bet he had a comment about our being together."

"He did. He warned me about getting in too deep."

"I hope you told him to mind his own business?" Blake's tone was crisp.

"He has got a point, though, hasn't he?" Carrie turned her face towards the sea.

"I would have thought getting in too deep was the only way to reach someone's heart." Blake took her hand, leading her towards the hard-packed sand. Waves were rolling into the beach, and a big, burnished moon was riding high.

Carrie waited a moment to answer. "But then the price of love can be great. You know that. My poor father does. Life has become unbearable for him without my mother."

"I recognize that, Carolyn."

"It's taken a long time for you to get over Amanda."

Blake's reaction was unexpected. In one fluid movement he turned her towards him, his hands ungentle. "What's stirred all this up?"

"Oh, seeing you among friends."

"You mean Diane?"

Despite herself, her body flowed to him. "I'm afraid I overheard a little of your conversation."

"How is that?"

"I was coming to find you," she answered simply.

"So Diane had a bit too much to drink," he suggested.

"She's in love with you."

"Oh, rubbish!" His voice was irritated in the extreme.

"Anyway, it's your business." Carrie tried to break away, but he was too strong.

"You don't believe me? Look at me, Carolyn."

"How did she get to that stage?"

"You seem to have overheard an awful lot." His voice was cool to the point of cutting.

"It was ill-advised. Not illegal."

"Let's settle this right now," he said angrily. "There is no way, no way I could approach you, make love to you if I was having a relationship with Diane."

"Something happened, Blake. I can tell."

"You can't tell anything!" he responded with hard impatience. "The best you can do is talk nonsense."

"So, let's go home." Her voice broke.

"Not right now. If I'm going to be condemned on the basis of a few jealous words I might as well make it worthwhile." His fingers closed over her chin. "I want you. As well you know."

"Because you relish a challenge?"

There was a wild kind of excitement in resisting him. It lasted maybe a few seconds before Blake effectively checked her by placing both arms around her and drawing her tightly against his hard, muscled body.

"Is this smart, really, trying to provoke me?"

She tried another futile twist and turn. "I wouldn't have it any other way."

"There speaks the redhead. I knew it would be easy to arouse her." In a movement of spontaneous passion he moved into kissing her. She felt a mind-bending excitement that tore her defences apart. For a man's mouth to evoke such ecstasy, a feeling of exaltation! There was only one end to this. She was on fire, yet exquisitely pliant, at last realising to her shock that she was breathing endearments into his mouth. Secret things that affected him deeply, because he wrenched away, his voice vibrant with passion.

"This is all too easy for you, isn't it? You've kept me on the keen edge of desire for years. You know better than anybody how to get to me."

"Get to you?" Carrie protested almost brokenly. "Lord, when I feel so vulnerable, so open to you. I told you, when I'm with you, I'm a woman on the edge."

"So now you know I'm the same way. At least we've torn apart that pretence. There's only one thing. If you respond to me like you do in the course of this night, anything might happen. Passion carries its own burden."

Carrie lifted a trembling hand to her face. It was burning. "Do you think I don't know that? Caution is a frail thing when I'm with you."

There was one long, dangerous moment, then Blake drew back. "We'd better go," he said tonelessly, "before I completely lose my head."

It was almost a week before Carrie saw Blake again. A long week of hiding her inner anxieties in hard work. The message seemed to be that she had offended him bitterly. Perhaps their brief tempestuous affair was all over. Carolyn Donovan wasn't the kind of woman he wanted after all. She had too many inadequacies. Too many problems to sort out. When Blake finally did call he took her by surprise. She was in the vegetable garden gathering a basket of rich red tomatoes when Blake came through the white picket gate.

"Everything looks flourishing," he commented in his normal, assured voice. "You've inherited your mother's green thumb."

Carrie put up a hand to shade her eyes. The sun was strong, but she was more dazzled by Blake's sudden appearance. For all his elegance in formal clothes, this was the look she liked best. Tight-fitting jeans, a large buckled silver belt, an open-necked shirt, his Akubra tilted rakishly over his blue eyes, riding boots on his feet. She just managed not to sigh aloud. Instead she stood up. "Hi, Blake. I didn't think you remembered me."

"I thought I'd let you miss me."

"As a matter of fact I did." *You'll never guess how much,* she thought.

"Then we're both making progress." He looked into her upturned face. "I have to go over to Aurora at the weekend. I thought you might like to come. We'd need to stay overnight."

"Your cousin, Stuart, and his wife will be there?" She was so thrilled she said the first thing that came into her head.

He took the basket from her. "Carolyn, I'm getting sick of your high moral tone. Of course they'll be there."

"I always like to check out the sleeping arrangements." She smiled.

"I think you've got good cause to trust me. So, are you coming?"

"I'd love to," she said without reservation, so happy to see him she lost sight of every other consideration.

Aurora had belonged to the Courtlands since the mid 1860s, when Blake's great-great-grandfather, a wealthy young Englishman sailing around the world, dropped anchor in Middle Aurora's blue haven and decided to stay. The islands—there were three—continued to grow sugar and run prime dairy cattle to this day. Blake's cousin, Stuart, was in charge of operations and was responsible to Blake as chairman of Courtland Enterprises. As well as cattle and sugar, the family had interests in mining, land development, road transport and hotels. *Probably a lot more I don't know about,* Carrie thought. To be asked to Aurora was a great honour. She had never been there before. Another shopping trip was called for.

Only Fate intervened.

When Carrie returned from her shopping trip late Friday afternoon she found Blake waiting for her. The brothers, Frank and Ben, were sitting on the front steps, their heads in their hands. There was a profound silence over the plantation. All work had stopped.

She knew before she even stepped out of the Jeep something was terribly wrong. Blake was moving towards her, his face a tight mask.

Fear flew through her, a premonition of disaster. "It's Dad, isn't it?" She looked at him for support and confirmation.

"A heart attack in the field." Blake reached for her. "They've taken him away."

"Away?" She looked at him blindly. "Then I must go to him. Where is he?" She tried to control the great shudders that began to overtake her.

"Come into the house for a while, Carolyn," Blake urged. "You need something to calm you."

"No!" She shook her head emphatically. "He's in hospital, isn't he? I must go to him."

"Gawd, I can't take this!" Frank rose from the steps in extreme agitation. "What can anyone say to prepare her? Hasn't she had enough to bear?"

Carrie spoke blindly, in utter confusion. "He's not dead. He can't be."

"Carolyn, I'm so sorry." Blake's striking face bore the stamp of violent shock.

"It's not true!" She kept looking at him as if there were some dreadful misunderstanding, while Frank and Ben stood white-faced, mashing their bats between their hands.

She was aware Blake's arms tightened around her as she slumped. "But I love him. I want to tell him." Her whole body shook with a kind of sick impotence. "This isn't happening. Not both my parents." Even as she moaned her anguish, Carrie heard her mother's voice clearly.

"Carrie, my Carrie," the voice said.

The twins came home, stunned by this latest tragedy. It seemed the whole town turned out for the funeral, but Carrie could find no comfort anywhere. Why did some families have to suffer so much? she asked herself, knowing there were no answers.

Blake was a tower of strength, taking over all arrangements on Carrie's behalf. Mostly she sat on the veranda with her brothers talking about old times. Both young men did their best to show their love and comfort, but the grief was too great.

After about a week they were forced to leave. Both of them had been offered good jobs for the vacation, and they desperately needed the money. Blake drove them to the airport. Carrie stayed home. It was too much to have to wave them goodbye.

An hour later Blake returned to find Carrie still sitting on the veranda staring desolately into space.

"You can't stay here." He dropped into a chair beside her.

"This is my home."

"And you can't stay in it alone," he said more firmly. "I couldn't have that on my mind. Come over to me for a while. I'll have Aunt Evie stay."

Carolyn turned her head. "That's very kind of you, Blake, but I don't think so. I want to be on my own."

"Then that presents a problem. For me and for you. The farm is too isolated. Anyone could come in off the road. Lord knows there are enough drifters passing through the North. I don't like it at all. Your father wouldn't have liked it, either."

"Why didn't we know he had a bad heart?" Carrie asked in a dull voice.

"A number of factors went into that massive heart attack, Carolyn. Your father didn't care about life. Not after your mother died. He just wanted it over."

"At fifty-two?" She gave a little laugh that broke.

"I know." He, too, sounded bone-weary. "You tried very hard to look after him, but he set you an impossible task. We all make our own choices in life. Besides, who knows? Your mother and father could well be reunited. It's all he wanted."

Carrie was without voice. It was perfectly true.

CHAPTER FIVE

WEEKS passed. Christmas came and went. Carrie went through all the motions, but inside she felt her heart had turned to stone. Nevertheless, because she was young and being cared for, there were compensations, brief moments of peace and communing with nature. She had always had a sense of homecoming whenever visiting Courtland Downs. Living there allowed her to fully appreciate its extraordinary freedom and beauty.

Blake's Aunt Evie had come to stay. Eve Courtland had never married, choosing a career as an anthropologist. Now, in retirement, she was still keeping up her writing career. Evie was there when Carrie had need of her company, but Evie did her own thing, allowing Carrie much-needed space.

Soon she would have to pick up the broken strands of her life. Stand on her own two feet. In her sad limbo she had accepted far too much of Blake's time and endless generosity. The plantation had sold almost at once. A neighbour had bought it, planning to incorporate it into his own plantation. When their financial position was finally known, Michael Donovan's three children had to come to terms with the fact there would be very little left over for them. In four short years Michael Donovan had lost so much it staggered them. All they could do was accept it.

Late in January, Blake left for Japan for a round of business talks that was expected to last several days. It was then Diane Anthony saw her chance to visit

Courtland Downs on the pretext of paying her respects to Miss Courtland, the distinguished anthropologist.

As luck would have it, on the very day Diane drove up to the front door of the homestead Evie had left an hour earlier to conduct some business in town.

Carrie was half asleep by the pool when Diane walked down from the terrace.

Carrie sat up quickly, reaching for her cover-up. "What an unexpected surprise, Diane." She gestured for Diane to sit down.

"Actually I came to see Miss Courtland." Diane's eyes were cool. "Marvellous woman! So distinguished yet so approachable."

"Unfortunately she's gone into town."

"My sympathies about your father," Diane said. "You're an orphan now."

"I'm feeling it, Diane."

"I have to say you're looking a lot better than I expected." She stared at Carrie's beautiful face and body.

"I'm being very well cared for."

"I can imagine, but it has to stop. People are beginning to talk, of course. I say leave you in peace, but you know what people are like. Blake's everyone's idol. He wouldn't be Blake if he weren't so madly kind and generous, but all good things have to come to an end. What are your plans?"

Carrie looked at the cobalt blue sky. She didn't respond, so Diane rattled on.

"I know you wouldn't want to stay here. So many terrible memories. Wouldn't you be happier close to your brothers? Someone told me they've grown very handsome."

In her mind Carrie was praying fervently Evie would come back.

"Diane, what's really on your mind? You didn't come to see Evie, did you? You knew Blake was away. You wanted to see me."

"Actually, yes," Diane conceded with a tight smile. "It's perfectly obvious you have no one to advise you. If you don't know better yourself, someone has to tell you. It's time for you to move out. Blake is much too kind to say so, but your continuing presence must be becoming a burden. He doesn't entertain as he used to. He's been too busy sheltering little old you. Don't think I'm unsympathetic towards you. I know the awful time you've had, but you have to concede you're complicating Blake's life, whether you want to or not."

Carrie could feel her composure begin to leave her. "None of this is for you to say, Diane," she managed to reply. "I realise I'm at the end of my stay at Courtland Downs. My griefs haven't healed. They never will, but I'm stronger."

"Good. Then you do have some pride. Tell me, will you go to Brisbane to be with your brothers?"

Slowly Carrie got to her feet. "I'm not telling you anything, Diane. I can feel your hostility."

"I'd be hostile towards anyone who tried to take Amanda's place," Diane said angrily. "And you have pursued Blake, haven't you? Even now, playing the little victim. Amanda will always be there to come between Blake and any other woman. Any other woman, that is, but me. He's been taken up with you for a while. You're beautiful in an unconventional way, but once you're gone, Blake and I will be back to where we left off. He was on the verge of asking me to marry him before you put in your little play."

Carrie stared into the other girl's face, feeling unaccountably sorry for her. "Daydreams, Diane. Fantasies spun of your own desires. I know all about them."

"So why did he make love to me?" Diane suddenly challenged. "Yes, it's true!" Her eyes flashed. "He was alone a long time. So he called me Amanda in the night. In the morning, he knew. That's the point. I was there."

Carrie turned away, feeling sick to her stomach.

By the time Blake arrived home, well pleased with the outcome of his trip, Carrie had herself firmly in hand. As Diane had so kindly pointed out, she had overstayed her welcome. Her only excuse was that her multiple griefs had left her adrift. She didn't have much left in this world, but she did have her self-esteem. No one could take that from her but herself. She would tell Blake she intended to visit her brothers and then get herself a job. What sort of a job she didn't yet know.

She was very quiet at dinner and excused herself early, saying she had a slight headache.

Blake followed her into the hallway. "If you're up to it I'd like to show you something in the morning. We can't take the horses this time. It will have to be the four-wheel drive."

"When do we leave?" Her heart ached at the sight of him. Just as she thought she was drained of all feeling, the tumult started up again.

"Say after breakfast. That will give you a chance to sleep in."

By nine o'clock they were deep into the hinterland. After so much rain, the countryside was incredibly lush. Every watercourse was full-flowing, with beautiful native lilies adorning the serpentine banks. The land was clothed in luxuriant tropical vegetation. Palm trees soared among tall and graceful rainforest trees. There were groves of cabbage palms, pandanus, the native grass trees and the giant banyans. The further out they got, the grander the scenery became. They were in the middle of a blossoming Eden.

As they neared the most easterly tip of the spur Blake stopped the Jeep. "We'll walk in from here."

Beautiful savanna butterflies led the way, splashes of brilliant enamelled colours against the green woodlands. Carrie didn't see the entrance until they were upon it. Ancient cycads vied with magnificent tree ferns to screen an imposing arched opening that reminded her of a Gothic window. She watched with caught breath as Blake reached forward and removed the spent woody fibres of the tree ferns that draped the entrance like some intricately woven golden curtain.

"I'd say it was a lava tube from the old Kaloona volcano," he said quietly, taking her elbow. "The heavy run-off has caused the roof to collapse in several places. It won't be dark. The roof is exposed about one hundred feet on. You can see the blue sky."

"Lord," Carrie whispered, her voice full of reverence.

It was like entering some fantastic temple, majestic, colossal. The walls, ochre, rust-red, orange, black and chalky white, glittered as though studded with precious stones. The floor was a magnificent corridor of very fine red sand scattered with strangely shaped rocks, no two the same. Up ahead sunlight poured down in a giant laser beam, creating an awesome effect.

Carrie felt a wave of wonder pass through her. "This is a dream!" she said, hearing her voice echo. "One of nature's great miracles."

"It'll excite tremendous interest when I report it," Blake agreed with intense satisfaction. "It probably evolved from the time of Godwana."

Carrie looked up at the massive basalt walls. "So what are we talking about? A couple of hundred thousand years?"

Blake touched a gentle hand to the deep, deep grooves that must have marked lava flows. Thousands of lava drips hung from them like trickling candle wax. "Undara in the Gulf of Carpertaria was undisturbed for one hundred and ninety thousand years. I can't think we'll rival that, but this looks pretty impressive. We won't go in too far. It has to be checked out by the geologists first. There appear to be a series of caves and arches. I took the Cessna up to check the topography. So far you and I are the only ones to know about it."

"How splendid!" Carrie murmured, a flame of awe on her face. "You'll be the custodian, Blake. You and your heirs."

"It's a big responsibility," he agreed, looking towards the top of the dome. "There's a fragile ecosystem to be protected."

"Then you're the man for it." Carrie walked towards the column of golden light. "I'm honoured you showed it to me."

"You're welcome," he called after her, sounding a little amused. "Why so serious all of a sudden?"

Carrie turned and looked at him. "Perhaps I sense I might not see it again," she said quietly.

In an instant Blake's expression changed. It became high-mettled, as though challenged.

"That sounds ominous. What do you mean?"

She stared at him, this man who had become her life. "I've been thinking, I've imposed on you long enough."

"Damn that," he said, as though she had shaken him to the soul. "How do you begin to use the word imposition between us?"

"Isn't it?" Carrie argued, when her whole body was filled with physical longing. "I know it. You know it. The whole district knows it."

He made a small sound of contempt. "Should that worry us? God knows you've been very properly chaperoned."

"It's you I'm thinking about," she cried. "People never pass up the chance to talk."

"So, we can take care of that." He reached her in seconds, drawing her directly beneath the stream of golden light. "Carolyn Elizabeth Donovan," he said in a deep, thrilling voice, "I'm asking you to marry me. I know it's too early to talk about a wedding so soon after losing your father, but I want us to become engaged."

For a moment Carrie had to clutch his arms to steady herself. She felt so light-headed she thought she could float. "Engaged?" Her voice wavered.

Blake's expression was taut to the point of being hawkish. "We'll have our own little ceremony right now. There's no way. No way I'm going to lose you."

Before she had time to summon up a word, a ring was on her finger. A diamond masterpiece, composed of an emerald-cut central stone flanked by baguettes. It flashed out a kaleidoscope of brilliant lights. She had never seen anything so glorious or so extravagant in her whole life. Would he do anything to protect her and offer her a secure life?

"Carolyn, what's the matter?" He turned her averted face to him.

"Isn't this more than you ever had in mind?" She gave a ragged laugh when her eyes were full of tears.

"Why do you talk like that? When you've become my obsession."

Her mind was in a turmoil. "But I'm afraid, Blake. Afraid you may be taking your responsibilities too far. Please tell me the truth. It all culminated in my father's death, didn't it? You feel sorry for me."

He let out a brief, scornful laugh. "Damn it, you've had a rough time. Anyone would feel sorry for you."

"But only you have become my shield."

"Without a moment's hesitation." His blue eyes flashed. "But if you think I'm proposing out of pity, you must be crazy. You're beautiful. Clever. Brave. Unswervingly loyal. You're also a bit of a hothead." He smiled teasingly. "But despite the fact you're smart, you still get things terribly wrong. This is what I *want*, Carolyn. Not some grand gesture. How could you possibly think that?"

"Because I've seen how you are, Blake," she cried emotionally. "Your kindness and concern. The way you've looked after me."

"I've looked after you because we belong together." Very gently he shook her. "There's no running away. I'd only come after you and bring you back home." There was finality in his voice.

"You want me that badly?" Carrie stared into his brilliant eyes.

"Carolyn, what's kept you from knowing it? Having you live with me in my home has been my greatest joy. And my greatest torment. You've felt it, too, even through your grief. I've waited as long as I can, but I want our future to be decided now. I want a wife. I want a woman I can take right into my heart. It's never been filled before."

"Not even by Amanda?" She had to speak openly, to clarify her thoughts.

"Amanda was a delight. I loved her. We'd been friends since our childhood. I was devastated when she was killed. But I hadn't foreseen *you*. There's always been something between us. Even when you were so young and so shy of me. The only answer was to wait." He dropped a full, deep kiss on her mouth.

"And Diane?" she whispered, when she was able.

"I might have known what this was all about." He sighed. "So Diane managed to get to you? She's like that. It may shock you to know Diane tried to wreck her own sister's happiness.''

It wasn't hard to believe. "So why do you tolerate her?" Carrie asked.

"You may well ask! But after Amanda was killed Diane was so genuinely stricken, so guilt-ridden I didn't have the heart to exclude her. It's only since she became aware of my feelings for you that she really started to unravel.''

"She told me you were lovers." Carrie held his gaze.

Blake's handsome mouth compressed. "Did you believe her?''

"No, I didn't. What I *did* believe was it was time I stopped complicating your life. Ever since Dad died, I've felt so vulnerable. You've become my protector.''

"You don't like it?''

"I must stand on my own two feet.''

"I wouldn't have it any other way. And you're good at it. But there are times when we all have to turn to someone for support. You've taken so much in your life. Yet despite everything you haven't snapped. You have to give yourself time to heal, Carolyn. We won't be able to live a quiet life once we're married.''

Married! She felt a wonderful surge of the life force through her blood. She was flushed with it. "But you haven't once said you loved me.''

"Oh, yes, I have!" He tilted her chin. "I've said it in a thousand different ways. I've shown it in everything I've done. I know you're in love with me, but I'm much further along than that.''

"How far?" Her voice was husky with yearning.

"You've transformed my life.''

"Go on." She slipped her arms around his neck, half drugged by enchantment.

"Not until you say yes." His brilliant eyes showered sparks.

"I'm wearing your ring."

"You are."

Now it's my turn, she thought. "I love you with all my heart," she began fervently. "I've loved you from the minute I knew what adult love was. *Before* that, but I didn't know about desire. I didn't know the physical agony of being apart. I didn't know the ecstasy of being together. I didn't know you wanted me for your wife. It was my impossible dream."

The sun turned her head into a dark, flaming glory. He lifted it, his face blazing with love and vitality. "But it's not a dream, Carolyn," he said. "It's very real. From this day forward, we embark on a new life."

EPILOGUE

IT WAS nearing the close of a brilliantly fine day. The month was May, a heavenly time in the tropics, when the weather was absolutely perfect. On this, her wedding day, Carrie stood before her wall of mirrors, a soft smile on her face, while Susan, her bridesmaid, fussed around her, telling her with every other breath how beautiful she looked. And it was beauty to the ultimate degree. Happiness had raised Carrie's beauty to breathtaking radiance.

A few feet away, her two adorable little flower girls, Camilla and Emma, six and four, blue-eyed blondes from the Paget side of the family, clapped their hands in excited anticipation of the helicopter trip ahead. The early photographic session had gone wonderfully well. Now they waited for the Courtland helicopter to return to ferry them to the island.

They were to be married on Aurora. Carrie and her splendid Blake. Everything was going beautifully, and it was Carrie who had planned it. Aurora was where it had all started. Where Blake's great-great-grandfather had had his own wedding. No one in the family had been married there since, but Blake had instantly accepted her suggestion as marvellous.

And so it had been arranged. Months and months of meticulous organization. It was apparent she had a flair for it.

"Oh, Carrie, I can't believe this!" Susan said, hugging her friend gently. "You and Blake! It's like a dream come true, and so wildly romantic. I'm so thrilled for you.

You truly deserve such happiness.'' Susan's golden-skinned, attractive face grew slightly pink. "Do you remember how I used to call Blake a god of the rainforest?''

The two friends locked eyes then broke into laughter. "It was always perfectly clear to me,'' Carrie said. "Blake is very special. A man apart.''

"All that fire! You have to be the luckiest girl in the world.''

"It certainly feels that way.'' Carrie looked at her reflection, unable to conceal her delight in her appearance. Happiness and excitement warmed her like rays of golden sunshine. This was such an extraordinary day. She had never felt remotely like this before. The joy and the great rushes of emotion. Blake meant everything in the world to her, and tonight they would come together for the very first time.

My perfect love, she thought, overjoyed. Their love was a miracle, deepening and intensifying with each passing day. She was going to do everything in her power to see that it endured forever. For an instant, her dreamy green eyes misted over, making her reflection in the mirror shimmer.

She wasn't wearing full regalia. That wouldn't have been appropriate for an island wedding, but her white wedding dress was everything a bride could wish for, an exquisite creation of rose guipure lace, the bodice tightly fitting, halter necked with a wasp waist over a marvellous, ankle-length organza skirt. Her white wedding shoes had been specially made for her, embroidered and decorated, a work of art in themselves. She didn't wear a veil because of all the sea breezes, but wore her mother's wedding headdress; a family heirloom sent from Ireland by a Donovan great-aunt at the time of her parents' wedding. Many a time her mother had allowed her to look at it and occasionally set it on her head while her mother and father looked on and exchanged loving smiles. For all the shortness and tragedy of her parents' lives, when it was considered they had truly known love. Her mother had always told Carrie she could wear the headdress on her wedding day, this delicate trembling diadem of gilded leaves, lustrous pearls and hundreds of tiny glittering crystals. Something the young Carrie had thought a fairy princess might wear. Now it adorned her head, trailing gleaming embroidered ribbons and a cascade of white butterfly orchids.

Susan and her small attendants were dressed in the same airy theme, taking the rich cream and yellow of the frangipani that was incorporated in their ravishingly pretty floral headdresses, Susan's bouquet and the flower girls' little baskets. Susan, a willowy brunette with a gleaming straight fall of hair, looked wonderful in yellow. The two little flower girls with their long flaxen hair and full shining fringes were dressed entirely in cream organza, embroidered in yellow on the puff sleeves and bodice, with wide yellow taffeta sashes to match Susan's gown. They looked utterly enchanting. Just to see them was to become wreathed in smiles.

Blake's gift to each flower girl was a beautiful little eighteen-carat gold unicorn of love with a full-cut diamond in its head, suspended from a delicate gold chain. A precious treasure for them to keep. Susan's gift was a necklet featuring a single radiant flower crafted of yellow sapphires and gold suspended from a matching chain. For his bride, Blake had chosen the lustrous timeless pearls Carrie loved. A single strand of the largest and finest pearls from the South Seas. There were earrings to match, an exquisite pearl set like a dome atop a sea of diamonds. They looked wonderful with her gleaming diadem, combining magnificently the very old with the newly created.

A short time later Carrie and her attendants were riding high in a peacock blue sky on their twenty-minute flight to Aurora Island. The view from the air was stupendous. Quite unforgettable. From the pale aquamarine of the harbour to the unbelievably blue sea scattered with emerald islands and hundreds of tiny coral cays crowded with bird life and surmounted on platform reefs. The Great Barrier Reef was one of the great wonders of the world. A continuous rampart of coral stretching twelve hundred miles and covering an area of some eighty thousand square miles. At its outer edge it plunged a hundred fathoms to the ocean floor, a factor that had warded off the Spanish, the Portuguese and the French on their epic journeys into unknown waters. It was Captain James Cook, flying the British flag, who had finally managed to navigate the perilous waters of the reef, and even he had almost met with disaster. Carrie had only seen the Outer Reef once in her lifetime. It was very difficult to see, and then only at the right time. She and her father had cruised for more than a day, awestruck by the huge, tumultuous surf rising out of an unbroken flat ocean. The next morning when the tide was at its lowest point they had walked the phenomenal coral gardens. It was one of her most vivid memories. She remembered it now, swallowing the little lump in her throat.

As they approached Aurora Island Carrie felt a great leap of the heart. This was magic, and she had to fight back the waves of emotion so near the surface on this day of all days. Aurora rose sheer from the water, at its centre a flat-topped mesa covered in virgin rainforest from which a shimmering waterfall flowed. Coral sand of sun-drenched whiteness ringed the island around. Its turquoise lagoon was of such translucent purity it was possible to see the sea floor. There couldn't have been a more exciting way to arrive, a trip more breathtaking.

Even as they looked down they witnessed with delight the arrival of a school of dolphins into the lagoon, causing the little girls to cry out in a near ecstasy of enchantment.

"Messengers of the gods, Carrie!" Susan called, her eyes sparkling. "It's a good omen."

In another few minutes they would be landing on the homestead's front lawn. Other guests had arrived in the same way, but many had decided to sail their marvellous yachts and motor cruisers into the beautiful blue lagoon. They were floating and bobbing like so many gigantic white waterbirds on the sparkling waters that turned into a collage of cerulean, aqua, then palest jade near the strand.

The ceremony was to be held on the beach with the glorious blue sea all around them. Carrie could see the covered walkway she would take, the specially designed and decorated archways festooned with flowers. White Moroccan canopies shaded the long reception tables, set at intervals with silver ice buckets of white liliums and tall bronze candelabra. Elegant white fitted covers had been made for the chairs, adorned at the sides with large silk rosettes. Carrie had found the most marvellous caterer to fulfill her fantasy of a wedding feast, a woman of impeccable style. A special feature of the banquet would be all the wonderful, succulent bounty of the reef waters around them. The whole menu was mouth-watering, but Carrie knew she would be too excited to eat much.

Organizing all the flowers had been her special delight. Flowers, and lots of them, created their own lovely atmosphere. White was the ultimate expression of this very special day, so as much as possible Carrie had chosen white roses, liliums, stephanotis, gardenias and orchids, as well as lots of soft blues and creamy yellow. She and her floral designer had tried dozens of shapes of bouquets against herself before they had finally decided on her exquisite bouquet introducing pinks and yellows and splashes of greenery to enhance the photography. Musicians would play from the homestead's veranda, and a member of the Courtland family, a famous soprano, was to sing. Neither of them had wanted a large wedding. There were plans for a gala occasion when they returned from their honeymoon in Venice. Only sixty of their closest friends and family had been invited. Sean and Steven were to give her away. A twin for each arm.

Towards late afternoon, as Carrie, fragrant bouquet in hand, stood beneath the beautiful flower-decked archway exchanging vows with her beloved Blake, something quite rare and wonderful happened. There was a green flash on the horizon. It lit up the rose, amethyst and gold of the sunset, causing many a guest's eyes to glaze over with tears. There was a scientific explanation. There always is, but Blake and Carrie, looking deeply into one another's eyes, took it for what it was. A blessing from above.

It was a flawless moment. Flawless. Blake, blazingly handsome in a suit of sand-coloured linen with a pin-tucked white shirt of the finest lawn and a perfect white camellia as a boutonniere, looked down on his bride as though spellbound by her beauty.

"I'll remember this moment *forever*," he said in a low, vibrant voice, then bent his head over Carrie's for the ceremonial bridal kiss.

His eyes had never been so brilliant, Carrie thought, returning her husband's loving embrace. They shone on her. Shone.

This was the most wonderful day of her life. A day of overwhelming happiness. Yet she knew in her heart the best was yet to come.

If you are looking for more titles by

MARGARET WAY

Don't miss these fabulous stories by one of
Harlequin's most renowned authors:

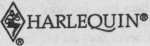

Take 4 bestselling love stories FREE

Plus get a FREE surprise gift!

Free Gift Offer

As Seen on TV!

With a Free Gift proof-of-purchase
from any Harlequin® book, you can receive
a beautiful cubic zirconia pendant.

This stunning marquise-shaped stone is a genuine cubic
zirconia—accented by an 18" gold tone necklace.
(Approximate retail value $19.95)

Send for yours today...
compliments of ◈ HARLEQUIN®

To receive your free gift, a cubic zirconia pendant, send us one original proof-of-purchase, photocopies not accepted, from the back of any Harlequin Romance®, Harlequin Presents®, Harlequin Temptation®, Harlequin Superromance®, Harlequin Intrigue®, Harlequin American Romance®, or Harlequin Historicals® title available in August, September or October at your favorite retail outlet, together with the Free Gift Certificate, plus a check or money order for $1.65 U.S./$2.15 CAN. (do not send cash) to cover postage and handling, payable to Harlequin Free Gift Offer. We will send you the specified gift. Allow 6 to 8 weeks for delivery. Offer good until October 31, 1996 or while quantities last. Offer valid in the U.S. and Canada only.

Free Gift Certificate

Name: _____

Address: _____

City: _____ State/Province: _____ Zip/Postal Code: _____

Mail this certificate, one proof-of-purchase and a check or money order for postage and handling to: HARLEQUIN FREE GIFT OFFER 1996. In the U.S.: 3010 Walden Avenue, P.O. Box 9071, Buffalo NY 14269-9057. In Canada: P.O. Box 604, Fort Erie, Ontario L2Z 5X3.

FREE GIFT OFFER   084-KMF

ONE PROOF-OF-PURCHASE

To collect your fabulous FREE GIFT, a cubic zirconia pendant, you must include this original proof-of-purchase for each gift with the properly completed Free Gift Certificate.

084-KMF

**This summer, the legend
continues in Jacobsville**

Diana Palmer

A LONG, TALL
TEXAN SUMMER

Three **BRAND-NEW** short stories

This summer, Silhouette brings readers a special
collection for Diana Palmer's LONG, TALL TEXANS
fans. Diana has rounded up three **BRAND-NEW**
stories of love Texas-style, all set in Jacobsville,
Texas. Featuring the men you've grown to love from
this wonderful town, this collection is a must-have
for all fans!

*They grow 'em tall in the saddle in Texas—and
they've got love and marriage on their minds!*

Don't miss this collection of original Long, Tall Texans
stories...available in June at your favorite retail outlet.

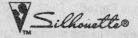

You're About to Become a *Privileged* *Woman*

Reap the rewards of fabulous free gifts and benefits with proofs-of-purchase from Harlequin and Silhouette books

Pages & Privileges™

It's our way of thanking you for buying our books at your favorite retail stores.

PROOF OF PURCHASE
HR-PP183
Offer expires October 31, 1996

**Harlequin and Silhouette—
the most privileged readers in the world!**

For more information about Harlequin and Silhouette's PAGES & PRIVILEGES program call the Pages & Privileges Benefits Desk: 1-503-794-2499

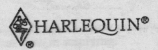